# VADA FRYE'S
# GHOSTS
# IN
# THE DARKNESS
# OF
# DESPAIR

## A
## J. Wayne Frye
## Anthology of Terror

**Teachers Should Advise Students That
This book is written in Canadian English**

# Vada Frye's Ghosts in the Darkness of Despair

**TO:**
Casey, Josh and Georgia
Gabe, Nicole and Jamie
Leah, Jolene and J.J.
(My grandchildren)

**AND AS ALWAYS, TO MY MUSE**
Lynton Viñas

Catalogue Number: 2016-2453599

ISBN:  978-1-928183-25-9

**Fireside Books – Victoria, British Columbia**
Part of the Peninsula Publishing Consortium

**J. Wayne Frye**

# Vada Frye's Ghosts in the Darkness of Despair

## TABLE OF CONTENTS

**Prologue…..5**
The Season of Ghosts
**Story 1…..9**
Gaskellian Darkness at the Manor House
**Story 2…..39**
La Fanu and the Strange Occurrence on Argyle
**Story 3…..57**
Howard and the Scurrying Blackbirds
**Story 4….. 95**
Lovecraft in the Forest of Despair
**Story 5…..105**
Horror With Cold, Icy Fingers
**Story 6….. 115**
Julius Long-Death Comes Calling
**Story 7 - 123**
William Hodgson's Demise
**Story 8…..139**
Mark's Ghost Story
**Story 9…..145**
Machen's March of Death
**Story 10…..153**
The Field of Poppies
**Story 11…..159**
The Church Bell
**Story 12…..167**
The Portrait of the Lady in the Velvet Gown
**Epilogue…..177**

# Vada Frye's Ghosts in the Darkness of Despair

## ABOUT THE AUTHOR
Wayne Frye's *Aaron Adams* mysteries, *Girl* series books and *Lynton* adventures have titillated the brains of those who enjoy tales that challenge the mind. His life, like those of the heroes he writes about, has been filled with adventure and excitement. He has been a college hockey coach, university professor, and at one time, the youngest university president in the USA. Called a marketing genius by the LOS ANGELES TIMES, he has been a promotional consultant to hockey teams and motion picture companies. He has been cited for his work with inner-city gang children in the Los Angeles area and been active in the anti-globalization movement. He weaves his tales at his beloved Bay View Château in Ladysmith, British Columbia, in sojourns in Laguna, Philippines and Cape Town, South Africa. He provides satirical political commentary to many Canadian newspapers, and his books on politics have created a great deal of controversy.

## Some Other Books by J. Wayne Frye

*Hockey Mania and the Mystery of Nancy Running Elk*
*Something Evil in the Darkness at Hopkins House*
*How Hockey Saved a Jew From the Holocaust*
*Fighting for Justice in the Land of Hypocrisy*
*The Girl Who Stirred up the Whirlwind*
*The Girl Who Motivated Murder Most Foul*
*The Girl Who Said Goodbye for the Last Time*
*Fall From Apocalypse*
*Armageddon Now*
*Worth*
*When Jesus Came to Jersey as the Son of Thunder*
*When Jesus Came to Canada to Lead an Indigenous Rebellion*
*When Jesus Came to the Black Hills to do the Ghost Dance*
*Canadian Angels of Mercy – Nurses in Times of Peril*
*Points of Rebellion: Aboriginals Who Fought for Justice*
*Lynton Curls Her Hair*
*Lynton Walks on Water*
*Lynton and the Vampire at Tagaytay Manor*
*Lynton Buys a Cell-Phone and Hears the Voice of Doom*
*Lynton Viñas and Beowulf Perez in the Taal Inferno*
*Lynton and the Ghosts at the Mansion on Balete Drive*
*Lynton Viñas: Shadow in the Darkness*
*Lynton's South African Adventure*
*Chablis: Avenging Angel for the Forgotten*
*Chablis and the Terrorist Who Resurrected the Spirit of Che*
*Chablis and Lynton in the Room of Doom*
*Pursuit*
The Disappearance

# Vada Frye's Ghosts in the Darkness of Despair

## Prologue
## The Season of Ghosts

For many people, the season of joy (Christmas) can often be one of despair. In a world where material things are promoted as the key to happiness, sometimes we lose sight of the true meaning of a time when family, love and compassion are supposed to take precedence over all other considerations. How strange that a day that is supposed to be promoted as a birthday celebration for a man who taught that the pursuit of material possessions was the root of all evil has morphed into a corporate money grab. Long ago, this holiday lost its meaning as the glitzy promotion of gifts was ballyhooed as the way to illustrate love.

It is appalling that most of us are taught as children to expect a cornucopia of Christmas gifts under a plastic tree to bring us happiness. The latest electronic gadgets, the finest clothes, the expensive toys, the glistening jewellery are all manifestations of how the true meaning of Christmas was long ago sacrificed at the altar of greed.

I was a materially fortunate child who watched his father claw his way out of poverty, but in the process material things for him seemed to often replace the real art of love that included the most valuable commodity of all – time. All the material things I received did not replace what I needed most – time with my father.

It was understandable that material things were important to my father and mother, because they both survived the Great Depression as children and experienced first hand the evil of an economic system that often crushed those at the bottom. However, my beloved grandmother never embraced the materialism of a society that saw Christmas, not so much as a holiday to celebrate the prince of peace, but as a holiday to promote buying things for people as an illustration of love and thereby fuel an obscene economic system that let most of the good flow to those at the top.

My dear grandmother, Vada Cranford Frye, rarely bought me any gifts, but she gave me the greatest gift of all – her time, and at Christmas her time was often spent telling me ghost stories. We would sit by the crackling fire as she would spin her tales of ghostly spectres and evil doings that titillated the mind of a young boy and motivated my love of ghostly literature.

Oral storytelling is a lost art today in a world of instantaneous entertainment dispensed by the technological marvels called the computer and smart phone. Alas, letter writing and story telling are seemingly tossed into the dustbin of history.

Do not misunderstand my intent. I am using a computer to write this book, so I grasp the modern world, though with some trepidation and reluctance. I embrace change, but I also lament what is often lost in the process of that change. A few years ago, after so many years of watching media miscreants prance about on reality television shows or listening to ridiculous laugh tracks to cue the viewer when to laugh at things that frankly were not funny, I decided that 350 channels of junk was still junk, so I got rid of television. I have no idea who the latest American Idol is. I have no idea whatsoever what the Kardashians are up to, or even what their first names might be. As for movie stars, I prefer movies without stars, because they generally have a story to tell rather than just blowing things up and using special effects to keep people from realizing those so-called stars are basically talent-less. I do not know who won the last super bowl. I have no idea who the NCAA basketball champions are, and frankly I consider myself better off for not knowing any of those things. I do not clutter my mind with the mundane.

I can tell you who the President of Poland is, and who is the Prime Minister of Australia. I can discuss Stephen Hawking's latest theories. I can speak a bit of Mandarin, though it generally elicits laughs from native speakers. I know where the

## Vada Frye's Ghosts in the Darkness of Despair

infamous Robben Island is and I can locate Pitcairn Island on a map and I know how long Nelson Mandela served in prison for standing against injustice. Also, I can actually tell an interesting story with proper inflections that will titillate the listener thanks to what I learned from my grandmother who was a master storyteller.

So, keeping all that in mind, with some modifications created by a faltering mind that cannot recall all the specifics, I share here with you as best I can recollect some of the harrowing tales of terror my grandmother shared with me at Christmas years ago that still caress me in the warmth of her love even today. Vada Cranford Frye is long gone, but the memories linger forever in the aging mind of a man who knew from her the real meaning of affection.

Vada was an uneducated woman, and not always articulate, so I must admit to some corrections to her grammar and a bit of fine tuning to her vocabulary, but each story is related pretty much as she told it to me.

## Story 1
## Gaskellian Darkness at the Manor House

You know Wayne I was just a girl in the New Hope village school, when, one day, a woman came in to ask the headmistress if there was any scholar there who would do for a nurse-maid; and mighty proud I was, I can tell you at the age of 12, when the mistress called me up, and spoke to my being a good girl at my needle, and a steady, honest girl, and one whose parents were very respectable, though they might be poor. I thought I should like nothing better than to serve the pretty, young lady, who was blushing as deep as I was, as she spoke of the coming baby, and what I should have to do with it. However, I see you don't care so much for this part of my story, so I'll skip some details.

I was engaged and settled in at the house which was in Denton, North Carolina, about 20 kilometres from where I lived. To be sure, I had little enough to do with the baby when she came, for she was never out of her mother's arms, and slept by her all night long; and proud enough was I sometimes when I was trusted with her. There never was such a baby before or since, though you have been a fine boy of course; but for sweet, winning ways, this was a fine baby, too. She took after her mother, who was a real lady and as fine a person as I ever knew. The woman got pregnant again within a couple of years. Ah, her husband was so delighted, but one day he came home feeling ill, took the fever and died. My poor mistress never raised her head in happiness again, and only lived long enough to see her baby born dead. As she lay dying, she asked me never to leave the child we called Rosebud.

Before we had well stilled our sobs, the executors and guardians came to settle the affairs. They were her cousin Fernell, and Edward, her brother, a shopkeeper in Asheboro; not so well to do then, as he was afterwards, and with a large family of his own. Well! I don't know if it was their settling, or because of a letter my mistress wrote on her death-bed to her cousin, but somehow it was settled that Rosebud and I were to go to Fernell's manor house in Denton, and off we went.

Fernell was a stern proud man, and he never spoke a word more than was necessary. Folks did say he had loved my young mistress; though as first cousins, they could not marry. He never married at any rate. Over time, he never took much notice of Rosebud, which I thought he might have done if he had cared for her dead mother so much.

On my 14th birthday, he sent me with Rosebud to set up housekeeping in an old mansion he had near the Uwharrie River. It seems like yesterday that we drove there. We had left our own dear manor very early, and we had both cried as if our hearts would break, though we were travelling in his new Essex automobile, which I thought was a grand experience.

It was long past noon on a September day, and we stopped by a small village now called Farmer which was full of miners. Rosebud, now six, had fallen asleep, but the chauffeur, Mr. Henry, told me to waken her, that she might see the park and her new home as we drove up. I thought it rather a pity; but I did what he bade me, for fear he should complain of me to Fernell. We had left all signs of a town, or even a village, and were then inside the gates of a large forested estate with huge rocks, and the noise of running water, and gnarled thorn-trees, and old oaks, all white and peeled with age. The road went up about two kilometres, and then we saw a great and stately house, with many trees close around it, so close that in some places their branches dragged against the walls when the wind blew; and some hung broken down; for no one seemed to take much care of the place.

The great oval drive was without a weed; and the house, although in a desolate place, was even grander than I expected. Behind it rose a tall hill, which seemed terribly barren, as if nothing would grow there at all; and on the left hand of the house, as you stood facing it, was a little, old-fashioned flower-garden, as I found out afterwards. A door opened out upon it from the west front, and all around were huge shade trees which made me wonder what flowers could grow there hidden from the sunlight. Ah, my query was answered, when I saw a few purple primrose flowers there in the shade, their eerie colour seeming to weep with despair and loneliness.

When we drove up to the great front entrance, and went into the hall I thought we should be lost - it was so large, and vast, and grand. There was a chandelier all of bronze, hung down from the middle of the ceiling; and I had never seen one before, and looked at it all in amazement. Then, at one end of the hall, was a great fireplace, as large as the sides of the living room where we sit now. At the opposite end of the hall, to the left as you went in - on the western side - was a huge pipe organ built into the wall, so large that it filled up the best part of that end. Beyond it, on the same side, was a door; and opposite, on each side of the fire-place, were also doors leading to the east front; but those I never went through as long as I stayed in the house, so I can't tell you what lay beyond.

The overall effect of the place, though grand in so many ways, was dark and gloomy, but we did not stay there a moment. An old servant, who had opened the door for us bowed to Mr. Henry, and took us in through the door at the further side of the great organ, and led us through several smaller halls and passages into the west drawing-room, where he said that Fernell's aunt was sitting.

Poor little Rosebud held very tight to me, as if she was scared and lost in that great place, and as for myself, I was not much better. The west drawing-room was very cheerful-looking, with a warm fire in it, and plenty of good, comfortable furniture about. Fernell's aunt was an old lady, not far from eighty, I should think. She was thin and tall, and had a face full of fine wrinkles with deep furrows. Her eyes were very watchful to make up, I suppose, for her being so deaf as to be obliged to use an old-fashioned cone she put in her ear to listen better. Sitting with her was a Mrs. Stark, her maid and companion, and almost as old as she was. She had lived with her ever since they both were young, and now she seemed more like a friend than a servant. She looked so cold, and grey and stony, as if she had never loved or cared for any one; and I don't suppose she did care for any one, except her mistress; and, owing to the great deafness of the latter, Mrs. Stark treated her very much as if she were a child. Mr. Henry gave some message from Fernell, and then he bowed goodbye to us all, taking no notice of my sweet little Rosebud's outstretched hand and left us standing there, being looked at by the two old ladies through their spectacles.

I was glad when they rang for the butler who had shown us in at first, and told him to take us to our rooms. So we went out of that great drawing-room, and into another sitting-room, and out of that, and then up a great flight of stairs, and along a long hallway, which was something like a library, having books all down one side, and windows and writing tables all down the other until we came to our rooms, which I was just over the kitchen below. There was an old nursery that had been used for all the children now grown, with a pleasant fire burning in a huge fireplace, and in the far corner was a tiny bed for Rosebud I assumed. And the butler, named James, came in and introduced his wife Dorothy. They were both so hospitable and kind, that by and by Rosebud and I felt quite at home; and before long Rosebud was sitting on Dorothy's knee, and chattering away as fast as her little tongue could go. James had lived pretty nearly all his life there, and thought there was no one so grand as the people he loyally served. He even looked down a little on his wife; because, until he had married her, she had never lived in any but a poor tenant farmer's household. Still you could sense his fondness for her.

They had one servant under them to do all the hard work. Agnes they called her; and she and I, and James and Dorothy, with Fernell's Aunt Matilda and her friend Mrs. Stark, made up the household. Oh, and how they all seemed to love little Rosebud. I often wondered what they had done before she came; they thought so much of her. Kitchen and drawing-room, it was all the same. The hard, sad Aunt Matilda, and the cold Mrs. Stark, looked pleased when she came fluttering in like a bird, playing and prancing all about, with a continual murmur, and pretty prattle of gladness. I am sure they were sorry many a time when she flitted away into the kitchen, though they were too proud to ask her to stay with them, and were a little surprised at her taste; though to be sure, as Mrs. Stark said, it was not to be wondered at, remembering what stock her father had come from, which I deduced to mean he was not very well bred by their standards.

The great, old rambling house was a fabulous place for little Rosebud. She ran with delight all over it, with me at her heels; all, except the east wing, which was never opened, and where we never thought of going. The darkness of the place though sometimes became a bit despairing, as every single window was darkened by the sweeping branches of the trees, and the ivy which had overgrown them, but, in the darkness, we managed to find joy in the exuberance of youth.

Once, I remember, Rosebud would have Dorothy go with us to tell us who all the people in the pictures hanging on the walls were; for they were all portraits of family, though Dorothy could not tell us the names of every one. We had gone through most of the rooms, when we came to the den over the hall, and there was a picture of Matilda; or, as she was called in those days, Missy, for she was the younger of two sisters. Such a beauty she must have been, but with such a prideful look, and such scorn looking out of her dark eyes, with her eyebrows just a little raised, as if she wondered how any one could have the impertinence to look at her; and her lip curled at us, as we stood there gazing. She had a dress on, the like of which I had never seen before, but it was all the fashion when she was young: a hat of some soft, white feathers as if from an albino peacock, pulled a little over her brows, and a beautiful plume of coloured feathers sweeping around it on one side; and her gown of blue satin was displaying just a small bit of cleavage.

Now, I could be impertinent myself at times, so I blurted out, "Wow, hard to believe Aunt Matilda was once such a beautiful woman. Age certainly does make alterations to our looks."

"Yes," said Dorothy. "Folks change sadly. But if what I hear is true, Miss Louise, the elder sister, was handsomer than Miss Matilda. Her picture is here somewhere; but, if I show it you, you must never let on, even to James, that you have seen it. Can the little lady hold her tongue?" she asked.

I was not so sure, for she was such a little, sweet, bold, open-spoken child, so I set her to hide herself; and then I helped Dorothy to turn a great picture that leaned with its face towards the wall, and was not hung up as the others were. To be sure, it beat Matilda for beauty; and, I think, for scornful pride, too, though in that matter it might be hard to choose. I could have looked at it an hour, but Dorothy seemed half frightened at having shown it to me, and turned it around again, and bade me run and find Rosebud, for that there were some ugly places about the house, where the child should not go. I was a brave, high-spirited girl, and thought little of what the old woman said, for I liked hide-and-seek despite my age, so off I ran to find my Rosebud.

As winter drew on, and the days grew shorter, I was sometimes almost certain that I heard a noise as if some one was playing on the great organ in the hall. I did not hear it every evening; but, certainly, I did very often; usually when I was sitting with Rosebud, after I had put her to bed, and keeping quite still and silent in the bedroom. Then I used to hear it booming and swelling away in the distance. The seventh night, when I went down to my supper, I asked Dorothy who had been playing music, and James said very shortly that I was just hearing the howling wind, but I saw Dorothy look at him very fearfully, and the cook, Agnes, said something beneath her breath, and went quite white. I saw they did not like my question, so I held my peace until I was with the more amenable Dorothy alone, when I knew I could get a good deal of information out of her. So, the next day, I watched my time, and I coaxed and asked her who it was that played the organ; for I knew that it was the organ and not the wind. However, Dorothy was dismissive of me and said not to meddle into things that were none of my business.

I tried Agnes. She said I must never ever tell; and if I ever told, I was never to say she had told me; but it was a very strange noise, and she had heard it many times, but most of all on winter nights, and before storms; and folks did say, it was the old master of the house, Fernell's grandfather, playing on the great organ in the hall, just as he used to do when he was alive; but why he played, and why only on stormy winter evenings in particular, she either could not or would not tell me. Well, I told you I had a brave heart; and I thought it was rather pleasant to have that grand music rolling about the house, even if played by a ghost.

As time went on and storms became more frequent, so did the organ playing. It would rise above the great gusts of wind, and wailed and triumphed just like a living creature, and then it fell to a softness most complete; only it was always music, and tunes, so it was nonsense to call it the wind, and not being a believer in ghosts, despite my comment to Agnes, I thought at first, that it might be Matilda who played, unknown to Agnes; but, one day when I was in the hall by myself, I opened the organ and peeped all about it and around it, and I saw it was all broken and destroyed inside, though it looked so grand and fine; and then, though it was day-time, my flesh began to creep a little, and I shut it up, and ran away quickly upstairs to my room; and I did not like hearing the music for some time after that, any more than James and Dorothy did. All this time Rosebud was making herself more and more beloved. The old ladies liked her to dine with them at their early dinner; James stood behind Matilda's chair, all through dinner as if he was a slave to

# Vada Frye's Ghosts in the Darkness of Despair

Aunt Matilda's needs, which I suppose he was, since those born into privilege expect others to bow in supplication to them. Not every poor person is like your grandmother, who does not bow before anyone be they king, queen or lowly beggar.

As I said, Matilda was so sad, and Mrs. Stark so dull; but Rosebud and I were merry enough; and, by-and-by, I got not to care for that weird rolling music, which did one no harm, even if we did not know where it came from. Still, in the back of my mind, there was always a question as to why and who was playing.

That winter was very cold. In the middle of October the frosts began, and lasted many, many weeks. I remember, one day at dinner, Aunt Matilda lifted up her sad, heavy eyes, and said to Mrs. Stark, "I am afraid we shall have a terrible winter," in a strange kind of meaning way. But Mrs. Stark pretended not to hear, and talked very loud of something else.

Rosebud and I could have cared less about the coming winter. As long as it was dry we clamoured about behind the house, and went up on barren hill where nothing ever seemed to grow, which was bleak, and bare enough, and there we ran races in the fresh, sharp air; and once we came down by a new path that took us past the two old, gnarled holly-trees, which grew about half-way down by the east side of the house. But the days grew shorter, and shorter; and the old ghost, if it was he, played away more, and more stormily and sadly on the great organ. One Sunday afternoon, it must have been towards the end of November, I asked Dorothy to take charge of little Rosebud when she came out of the drawing room, after Matilda had her nap; for it was too cold to take her with me to church, and yet I wanted to go, not so much as a believer, but just a curious person who loved to sample knowledge, and I always got a kick out of the preacher there, who was more interested in scaring people about going to hell than telling them about the glory of heaven. I found it most entertaining, as the congregation sit in fear, some actually shaking.

Anyway, Dorothy was glad enough to take care of Rosebud, as she was so fond of the child that all seemed well, and Agnes who had grown fond of me, and I set off very briskly for church with the sky hanging heavy and black overhead, as if the night had never fully gone away; and the air, though still, was very biting and seemed to penetrate us with a chill up and down our spines.

"We shall have a fall of snow," said Agnes to me. And sure enough, even while we were in church, it came down thick, in great, large flakes, so thick it almost darkened the windows. It had stopped snowing before we came out, but it lay soft, thick and deep beneath our feet, as we tramped home. Before we got to the hall the moon rose, and I think it was lighter then, what with the moon, and what with the white dazzling snow than it had been when we went to church, between two and three o'clock.

## Vada Frye's Ghosts in the Darkness of Despair

When I got back, I went to Dorothy in the kitchen to fetch Rosebud and take her upstairs with me. She said that Matilda and Mrs. Stark had kept the child with them. However, when I went into the drawing room, there sit the two old ladies, very still and quiet, dropping out a word now and then, but looking as if nothing so bright and merry as Rosebud had ever been near them. Still I thought she might be hiding from me, and that she had persuaded them to look as if they knew nothing about her. So, I went softly peeping under the sofa, and behind chairs, making believe I was sadly frightened at not finding her.

"What's the matter, Vada?" said Mrs. Stark sharply. I don't know if Matilda had seen me, for, as I told you, she was very deaf, and she sat quite still, idly staring into the fire, with her hopeless face. "I'm only looking for my little Rosebud," I replied, still thinking that the child was there, and near me, though I could not see her.

"Rosebud is not here, Vada" said Mrs. Stark. "She went away at least two hours ago to find Dorothy."

She then turned and looked into the fire. My heart sank at this, and I began to wish I had never left my darling little girl. I went back to Dorothy and told her. James was gone out for the day, but she, I and Agnes took lights and went up into the nursery first, and then we roamed over the great large house, calling and entreating Rosebud to come out of her hiding place, but she never answered our pleas – never came out.

# Vada Frye's Ghosts in the Darkness of Despair

Finally, I shouted, "Could she have gotten into the east wing and hidden there?"

Dorothy said it was not possible, for she herself had never been in there, and that the doors were always locked, and only Master Fernell had the keys, she believed; at any rate, neither she nor James had ever seen them. Thus, I frantically went back upstairs in a discombobulated state of mind to search again and again. I went back to the west drawing room, and I told Mrs. Stark we could not find her anywhere, and asked for permission to look all about the furniture there, for I thought now, that she might have fallen asleep in some warm, hidden corner; but no she simply had vanished. Matilda got up and looked, trembling all over, and she was no where there; then we set off again, every one in the house, and looked in all the places we had searched before, but we could not find her. Aunt Matilda shivered and shook so much that Mrs. Stark took her back into the warm drawing room; but not before they had made me promise to bring Rosebud to them when she was found.

Time passed by so terribly, aguishly slow I began to think she never would be found, when it occurred to me to look out into the great front court, all covered with snow. I was upstairs when I looked out; and, it was such bright moonlight, I could see quite plain two little footprints, which might be traced from the front door, and around the corner of the east wing. I don't know how I got down, but I tugged open the great, stiff front door;

and, throwing the skirt of my gown over head for a cloak, I ran out. I turned the east corner, and there a black shadow fell on the snow; but when I came again into the moonlight, there were the little footmarks going up toward the barren hill. It was bitter cold; so cold that the air almost took the skin off my face as I ran, but I ran on, crying to think how my poor Rosebud must be frightened, or worse - dead. I was within sight of the holly trees, when I saw a man coming down the hill, bearing something in his arms wrapped in his cloak. He shouted to me, and asked me if I had lost a child; and, when I could not speak for crying, he came towards me, and I saw my darling Rosebud lying still, and white, and stiff, in his arms, as if she was dead. He told me he had been up to the top of the hill looking for his sheep that were lost in the storm, before the deep cold of night came on, and that under the holly trees on the far side he had found Rosebud - stiff and cold, in the terrible sleep of fear.

I grabbed for her with tears streaming down my face like water over Niagara Falls. Having her in my arms once again was so joyous. I would not let him carry her as I held her near my own warm heart, and felt the life stealing slowly back again into her little, gentle limbs. Still, she was nearly comatose when we reached the house, and I had no breath for speech. We went in by the kitchen door, as I shouted for water to be boiled as I carried her upstairs and began undressing her by the nursery fire, which Agnes had kept up. I called my sweet Rosebud with pleas to awaken, as my eyes were blinded by my tears, and at last at length she opened her large, blue eyes. Then I put her into her warm bed, and sent Dorothy down to tell Matilda and Mrs. Stark that all was well; and I made up my mind to sit by my darling's bedside the live-long night. She fell away into a soft sleep as soon as her pretty head had touched the pillow, and I watched by her until morning light; when she wakened up bright and clear or so I thought at first.

She told me that the night before, while I was at church, that she had fancied that she should like to go to Dorothy in the kitchen, because both the old ladies were asleep, and it was very dull in the drawing room; and that, as she was going through the west lobby, she saw the snow through the high window falling soft and steady; but she wanted to see it lying pretty and white on the ground; so she made her way into the great hall; and then, going to the window, she saw it bright and soft upon the driveway; but while she stood there, she saw a little girl, not as old as she was, but so pretty, beckoning for her to come out, and so she did, and this little girl took her by the hand, and side by side the two had gone around the east corner. It was at this point that I said, "You are not to lie Rosebud. Do not compound things with lies."

She looked up at me with soulful eyes, almost pleading. "I am not lying my dear Vada. I am not lying I tell you. It is true. The little girl beckoned me to join her outside."

## Vada Frye's Ghosts in the Darkness of Despair

I was growing very angry with her for all the worry she had caused. I shouted at her, "Don't tell me such a lie. I tracked you by your foot marks through the snow. There were only yours to be seen, and if you had had a little girl to go hand-in-hand with you up the hill, don't you think the foot-prints would have gone along with yours?"

"I can't help it, Vada," she said, crying out in desperation, "I never looked at her feet, but she held my hand fast and tight in her little one, and it was very, very cold. She took me up the barren hillside, up to the holly trees on the far side and there I saw a lady weeping and crying; but when she saw me, she hushed her weeping, and smiled very proud and grand, and took me on her knee, and began to lull me to sleep; and that's all Vada, but it is true."

I thought the child was in delirium, and pretended to believe her, as she went over her story again and again always the same. At last Dorothy knocked with breakfast; and she told me the old ladies were down in the eating parlour, and that they wanted to speak to me. They had both been into the nursery the evening before, but it was after Rosebud was asleep; so they had only looked at her, not asked me any questions as I had fallen asleep in the chair beside Rosebud's bed.

"I shall catch it," I thought, as I went along the north gallery. And yet, I thought, taking courage, they had given me permission to go to church; and it was they who were of equal blame for letting her get out of sight.

# Vada Frye's Ghosts in the Darkness of Despair

So I went in boldly, and told my story. I told it all to Matilda, shouting it close to her ear; but when I came to the mention of the other little girl out in the snow, coaxing and tempting her out, and going with her to the holly tree on the far side of the hill, I hesitated, but thought it relevant, so I shared the detail in a dismissive manner. However, the reaction from them was not dismissive.

They both looked as if they had been slapped in the face with the cold hand of death. "Oh my," shouted Matilda as she stared at Mrs. Stark., and then took hold of my arm, squeezing it tightly. "Have mercy! Keep her from that child! It will lure her to her death! That evil child! Tell her it is a wicked, naughty child."

Then, Mrs. Stark, wrestled my arm from Matilda and hurried me out of the room; where, indeed, I was glad enough to go; but Aunt Matilda kept shrieking out, "Oh God, if you are indeed God, have mercy! Will you never forgive! It has been so long now."

I was very uneasy in my mind after that. I never left Rosebud, night or day, for fear she might slip off again, and all the more, because I thought I could make out that Aunt Matilda was crazy, from the odd ways about her. I was afraid night and day, as the great frost of winter never ceased, all this time; and, whenever it was a more stormy night than usual, between the gusts, and through the wind, we heard the great organ mournfully playing tunes.

**J. Wayne Frye**

# Vada Frye's Ghosts in the Darkness of Despair

Wherever Rosebud went, there I followed; for my love for her was stronger than my fears. So we played together, and wandered about together, here and there, and everywhere; for I never dared to lose sight of her again in that large and rambling house. And so it happened, that one afternoon, not long before Christmas day, we were playing together in the great hallway, as she liked to roll her many red rubber balls down the hallway, and, by-and-by, without our noticing it, it grew dusk indoors, though it was still light in the open air, and I was thinking of taking her back into the nursery, when, all of sudden, she cried out as she looked out the window at the end of the hall, "look, look Vada, there in the snow, she beckons again."

I rushed to the window, and there saw a little girl dressed all unfit to be out-of-doors on such a bitter night - crying, and almost pleading as if she wanted to be let in. She seemed to sob and wail, until little Rosebud could bear it no longer, turned and flew down the hallway and stairs as I ran frantically after her. As I took the stairs two at a time, all of a sudden, the great organ pealed out so loud and thundering it fairly made me tremble. Then I remembered that, even in the stillness of that dead-cold weather, I had myself now seen the phantom child and, although I had seen it wail and cry, I suddenly realized no faint touch of sound had fallen upon my ears. Whether I remembered all this at the very moment, I do not know; the great organ sound had so stunned me into terror;

but this I know, I caught up to Rosebud before she got the front door opened, and I clutched her with all my might, carrying her away, kicking and screaming, into the large, bright kitchen, where Dorothy and Agnes were standing in shock at all the commotion.

"What is the matter?" cried Dorothy, as I bore in Rosebud, who was sobbing as if her heart would break, saying "She won't let me open the door for my little friend to come in; and she'll die if she is out in this horrible weather."

Dorothy's face was as white as a sheet, emanating a fear that penetrated me like a lance. "Lock the back kitchen door fast, and bolt it well," said she to Agnes.

Agnes said nothing as she went to lock the door. We all took a seat and just stared at one another, until little Rosebud sobbed herself to sleep and I took her upstairs. As she fell into a deep sleep, I stole down to the kitchen, and told Dorothy I had made up my mind I would carry Rosebud back to Fernell's house away from all this. I said I had been frightened enough with the organ-playing; but now that I had seen for myself this little moaning child, all decked out as no child in the winter should be, begging and pleading to get in, yet always without any sound or noise – and what seemed a gapping wound on her right shoulder; and the fact that Rosebud had recognized it for the phantom that had nearly lured her to her death, I could not simply stand idly by any longer without bold action.

**J. Wayne Frye**

## Vada Frye's Ghosts in the Darkness of Despair

When I had finished, Dorothy told me she did not think I could take Rosebud away, for Fernell simply was not a man who abided children well. She insisted that he would simply send me back, dismissing me as a frightened child. Then, when I said I was through then and had to leave for my own sanity and that I did not sign on for a life grounded in fear, she asked if I could leave the child that I was so fond of, just for sounds and sights that could do me no harm.

I was all in a shaking, trembling state, and I said it was very well for her to talk, but she must know what these sights and noises were, and that she had, perhaps, had something to do with the phantom child while it was alive. And I taunted her so that she told me all she knew at last, and then I wished I had never been told, for it only made me more afraid than ever.

She said she had heard the tale from old neighbours that were alive long ago, when folks used to come to the manor sometimes, before it had gotten such a bad name in the country side. It might not be true, or it might, what she had been told. Fernell's grandfather was a very prideful man. Such a proud man was never seen or heard of anywhere else around there, and one of his sons (not Fernell's father) had two daughters (Matilda and her sister, Maude) who were like him. No one was good enough to wed them, although they had choice enough; for they were the great beauties of their day, as I had seen by their portraits, where they hung in the hallway. But, as the old saying is,

# Vada Frye's Ghosts in the Darkness of Despair

"pride goeth before the fall" and these two haughty beauties fell in love with the same man, and he was a honky-tonk playing musician, whom their father had up from Charlotte to play music with at several parties. For, above all things, next to his pride, the old man loved music. He could play on nearly every instrument that ever was heard of, and it was a strange thing it did not soften him; but he was a fierce, dour, old man, and had broken his poor wife's heart with his cruelty they said, which led her to finally just lie down and die to, as some believed, get away from him.

Anyway, he was mad after music, and would pay any amount of money for it. So he got this clarinet player to come; who made such beautiful music, that they said the very birds on the trees stopped their singing to listen. And, by degrees, this gentleman got such a hold over the old man that nothing would serve him but that he must come every so often. It was he who had the great organ made in Holland and brought to the house, and built to the music alcove, where it stood now. He taught the old man to play on it; but when the old man was thinking of nothing but his fine organ, and playing tunes on it, the musician was walking about in the woods with the young granddaughters, Maude and, of course, Matilda.

Maude won the day and carried off the prize, such as it was; and he and she were married, despite the old man's objections, and eventually Maud had a little girl in Albemarle where she had gone to live. Although she was a wife and a

**J. Wayne Frye**

mother, she was not a bit softened, but as haughty as ever; and perhaps more so for she was jealous of Matilda to whom her husband had paid far too much attention she felt. Maude grew fiercer and fiercer, both with her husband and with her sister; and the former who could easily shake off what was disagreeable, and hide himself in foreign countries where he was often booked to play, went away a month before his usual time that summer, and half-threatened that he would never come back again. Meanwhile, the little girl was left at a farm house beyond the barren hill behind the house with a woman who looked after her, as the old man wanted nothing to do with her and felt she was disruptive to the household. Maud would go see her once a week, but seemed distant. And the old man went on playing his infernal organ; and the servants thought the sweet music he made had soothed down his awful temper, of which some terrible tales could be told. He grew infirm too, and had to walk with a crutch; and his son, Fernell's uncle, was with the U.S. Army as a Colonel in places all over the world, where, as usual, America wanted to impose the culture of greed on other nations.

Maude had it pretty much her own way, and she and Matilda grew colder and bitterer toward each other every day, until at last they hardly ever spoke, except when the old man was around. The musician came again the next summer, but it was for the last time; for they made his life so miserable with their jealousy and their passions that he grew weary, and went away, and never was heard from again. Maude was left a deserted wife - with a child that she did not even acknowledge, although she loved it in her own way I suppose. Oh, her life was so miserable, living with a father whom she feared, and a sister whom she hated. When the next summer passed over and the musician never came, both Maude and Matilda grew gloomy and sad; they had a haggard look about them, though they were still beautiful.

Maude though was happier for her father grew more and more infirm, and more than ever carried away by his music, thus not bothering her as much. She and Matilda lived almost entirely apart, having separate rooms, Matilda on the west side, Maude on the east, those very rooms which are now shut up. So she thought she might have her little girl with her. As she was considering this, Matilda went into a tirade one day and told her that her husband had never loved her, but had always carried on an affair with her behind Maud's back. Mrs. Stark laughed with glee as Maud descended into tears. Matilda said with sullen intent that one day Maud would suffer the cruellest blow of all for stealing the man who really wanted her.

One fearful night, just after the New Year had come in, when the snow was lying thick and deep, and the flakes were still falling fast enough to blind any one who might be out there was a great and violent noise heard, and the old man's voice above all, cursing and swearing awfully, and the cries of a little child, and the proud defiance of a fierce woman, and the sound of a blow, and a dead stillness, and moans and wailing's dying away on the hillside. Then the old man summoned all his servants, and told them, with terrible oaths, and words that his daughter Maud was a disgrace, and that he had turned her out of doors, her, and her child, and that if ever they gave her help, or food, or shelter, he would fire them on the spot. And, all the while, Matilda stood by his side smiling with glee. The old man never touched his organ again, and died within the year; and no wonder, for, on the morning after he turned his daughter and granddaughter out, two men coming down the hillside found Maude sitting, all crazy and smiling, under the holly tree, holding a dead child, with a terrible wound on its right shoulder. The doctor said that the horrible wound, along with the bitter, biting cold on the hillside had done the child in.

I was more frightened than ever; but I said I was not. I wished Rosebud and myself out of that dreadful house forever; but I would not leave her, and I dared not take her away, but how I watched her and guarded her. I sternly bolted the doors, and closed the window shutters fast, an hour or more before dark, rather than leave them open five minutes too late, as I did not want to see the beckoning child. But my little Rosebud still sensed the weird child crying and mourning; and not all we could do or say, could keep her from wanting to go to her, and let her in from the cruel wind and the snow. All this time, I kept away from Matilda and Mrs. Stark, as much as I could; for I feared them. I knew no good could be about them, with their grey hard faces, and their dreary eyes, looking back into the ghastly years that were gone. But, even in my fear, I had a kind of pity for Matilda.

One night just after New Year's Day had come at last, and the long winter had taken a turn, I heard the west drawing room bell ring three times, which was the signal for me. I would not leave Rosebud alone, as I feared she should waken to sense the spectre child beginning to come in. You see, I knew in my heart why she wanted in.

On that night, I wrapped Rosebud up and carried her down to the drawing room, where the old ladies sat staring into space. They looked up when I came in, and Mrs. Stark asked, quite astounded, "Why did I bring Rosebud there, out of her warm bed?" I had begun to whisper, "Because I was afraid of her being tempted out while I was away, by the wild child in the snow," when she stopped me short (with a glance at Matilda), and said, "We need you to stoke the fire as Agnes and Dorothy are not about."

So, I went over and stoked the fire. Mrs. Stark drifted off to sleep as the wind howled outside. Matilda slept on soundly, as the wind blew furiously; and she was not roused to say a word, nor look around when the gusts shook the windows. All at once she started up to her full height, and put up one hand, as if to bid us listen.

# Vada Frye's Ghosts in the Darkness of Despair

"I hear voices!" said she. "I hear terrible screams. I hear my father's voice!"

Just at that moment, Rosebud awakened with a sudden start saying, "The little girl is crying, oh, how she is crying!"

She tried to get up and go to her, but she got her feet entangled in the blanket, and I caught her; for my flesh had begun to creep at the noises. In a minute or two the noises came, and gathered fast, and filled our ears with screams, and we no longer heard the winter's wind that raged about. Mrs. Stark looked at me, and I at her, but we dared not speak. Suddenly Matilda went towards the door, out into the ante-room, through the west lobby, and opened the door into the great hall. Mrs. Stark followed, and I dared not be left, though my heart almost stopped beating for fear. I wrapped Rosebud tight in my arms, and went out with them. In the hall the screams were louder than ever; they sounded as if coming from the east wing - nearer and nearer - close on the other side of the locked-up doors. Then I noticed that the great bronze chandelier seemed all alight, though the hall was dim, and that a fire was blazing in the vast fireplace there, though it gave no heat; and I shuddered up with terror, and pulled Rosebud closer to me. But as I did so, the east door shook, and she, suddenly struggling to get free from me, cried, "I must go! The little girl is there; I hear her; she is coming! I must go!"

I held her tight with all my strength; with a set will, I held her. If I had died, my hands would have grasped her still, I was so resolved in my mind.

Matilda stood listening, and paid no regard to Rosebud, who had gotten down to the floor, and whom I, upon my knees now, was holding with both my arms clasped round her body, as she still strived to get free. All at once, the east door gave way with a thundering crash, as if torn open in a violent storm, and there came into that broad and mysterious light, the figure of a tall, old man, with grey hair and gleaming eyes. He drove before him, with many a relentless gesture of abhorrence, a stern and beautiful woman, with a little child clinging to her dress.

"Oh Vada! Vada!" cried Rosebud. "It's the lady, the lady below the holly tree and the little girl is with her. Vada, Vada, let me go to her, they are drawing me to them. I feel them - I feel them. I must go!"

Again she was almost convulsed by her efforts to get away; but I held her tighter and tighter, until I feared I should do her a harm; but I could not let her go towards those terrible phantoms. They passed along towards the great hall door, where the winds howled and ravaged for their prey; but before they reached that, the lady turned; and I could see that she hated the old man with a fierce and proud defiance. Then he moved toward them, toward the child with raised crutch as the woman phantom threw her arms wildly and piteously to save her child - her little child - from a blow from his uplifted crutch.

**J. Wayne Frye**

# Vada Frye's Ghosts in the Darkness of Despair

And Rosebud was torn as by a power stronger than mine, and writhed in my arms, and sobbed as she cried, "No, no, do not hit her." The she turned to me and said, "I must go with them to the other side of the hill – to the holly tree."

She was trying desperately now to break free, and it was all I could do to hold her. She looked at me pleading. "They draw me to them, Vada. Please free me."

Suddenly, the crutch was about to come down full force upon the child and at that moment the tall, old man, his hair streaming as if lit by the very fires of hell itself, was going to viciously strike the little, shrinking child who was cowering in fear as Matilda, Mrs. Stark by her side, cried out, "Oh father, kill the little spawn of the devil!" But just then I saw, we all saw, another phantom forming itself, and grow clear out of the blue and misty light that filled the hall; we had not seen her until now, for it was another lady who stood by the old man, with a look of relentless hate and triumphant scorn. That young lady, the image of the young Matilda, grabbed the crutch from the father and swung it violently toward the woman with the child, but missed and hit the child on the right shoulder with full force. The poor child collapsed unconscious and her weeping mother picked her up and the two spectres quickly departed, disappearing through the front door, and the old man and the spectre of young Matilda moved back toward the formally locked rooms and disappeared into the darkness there.

## Vada Frye's Ghosts in the Darkness of Despair

I realized the real murderer of the child was Matilda as at that very moment, the dim lights, and the fire that gave no heat, went out and falling to the floor with a thud was old Matilda, without question, dead from fright! Justice was done, but in the process of justice, were two other great injustices. We would never know what happened to Maud, who was also probably murdered by Matilda, but Matilda had also claimed another victim on this night. You see, in my shivering arms, as a result of fear from all that had occurred, my dear Rosebud breathed no more.

J. Wayne Frye

**Vada Frye's Ghosts in the Darkness of Despair**

**Story 2**
**La Fanu and the Strange Occurrence on Argyle**

*My dear grandmother was pleased when I had a perplexed look on my face after she finished her story about the little girl ghost, as she so enjoyed seeing me think long and hard about a story she had spun. The purpose was not to just enthral me, but to make my young mind absorb information and develop my cognitive abilities. Though uneducated, she was a woman of immense wisdom and intelligence. She always encouraged me to write stories of my own and share them with her.*

*When some people would chastise me for reading murder mysteries by Mickey Spillane, which had an extremely generous helping of sex, she would tell my many detractors, "Let the boy alone. He is reading Mickey Spillane to refine his writing skills, and Mickey is an extremely good teacher of how to use words. I am but an old woman, but I, myself, find Mickey Spillane a grand weaver of tales."*

# Vada Frye's Ghosts in the Darkness of Despair

*One Christmas, I was particularly morose when I was sick. However, my mother and father still allowed me to spend the usual Friday night with my grandmother, and three days before Christmas, she sat in her rocker by the pot bellied stove which was whirring away dispensing a steady stream of heat on a cold night, as I pleaded with her for a scary story. She smiled and said, "You love a good tale almost as much as me boy. O.K., here we go with something that was once told me by a man named La Fanu."*

It is not worth telling, this story of mine, at least, not worth writing in many ways, but I shall still share it and let you decide. In fact, I get a bit weary telling it myself as I have sometimes been called upon to tell it to a circle of intelligent and eager faces lighted up by a good after dinner fire on a winter's evening, with a cold wind rising and wailing outside, while all were snug and cosy within, making it accepted sometimes with some indifference. But it is a venture to do as you would have me. Pen, ink and paper are cold vehicles for the marvellous, and a reader decidedly a more critical animal than a listener. I will spin it for you with delight my boy, and say my say, with happy heart. Well, then, these conditions presupposed, I shall waste no more words, but tell you simply how it all happened.

My cousin, Riley Hopkins, while I was attending high school, purchased three or four old houses on Argyle Street in Denton, one of which was unoccupied. He asked me to stay in one of the

J. Wayne Frye

houses he could not rent, so long as it should continue un-rented just so I could keep an eye on it. I was but 16 at the time, and thought it grand to be out on my own for even a short while on my summer vacation. I was a quiet and serene young girl, so I assumed it would allow me to, as the saying goes, spread my wings. Still, there was something about that old house that just didn't seem right.

The furniture was very scant, remarkably modest and primitive; and, in short, my arrangements pretty simple. The front drawing room was my sitting room. I had the bedroom over as the back bedroom on the same floor, for reasons which will become clearer, I simply felt I should avoid.

The house, to begin with, was a very old one. It had been, I believe, neglected for many years, and it had nothing modern about it. The agent who bought it and looked into the titles for Riley, dated it back to 1802, but could trace owners no further than that. In that year it was bought by a Thomas Hackett, who had come over from Ireland where he had been a politician, but not an honest one, as he was run out of the country. How old it was then, I can't say; but, at all events, it had seen years and changes enough to have contracted all that mysterious and saddened air, at once exciting and depressing, which belongs to most old homes that seem to simply reek of mystery. This one had a sinister air about it.

There had been very little done in the way of modernizing details on the house; and, perhaps, it was better so; for there was something quaint about the walls and ceilings, the shape of doors and windows, in the odd diagonal chimney, unusual carvings in the beams and ponderous cornices, not to mention the singular finery of all the woodwork, from the banisters to the window-frames.

An effort had, indeed, been made to the extent of papering the drawing-rooms; but, somehow the paper looked raw and out of keeping; and the old woman, who kept a little coffee shop on Main Street, often dropped by in the late afternoon to say hello, but she, for some reason, would never stay when it got dark. She remembered the home from a time when Judge Hackett (sometimes referred to as "Hanging Hackett") lived there and ended his own life in the house by hanging himself. It seems he had been driven over the edge by the sound of a child skipping-rope outside his home. He had complained to people about this on many occasions, and they just all began to think that he was slowly going mad, as what was wrong with some kid skipping rope? Anyway, irony upon irony, he actually hanged himself with a skip rope.

Getting back to the house when I was there, the front bedroom was actually cheerful, which is why I chose it. The back bedroom had two queerly-placed melancholy windows staring vacantly at the foot of the bed, a shadowy recessed alcove in a far corner, a huge ghostly closet and a large mirror that hung on the wall next to it. At night time, this alcove had, in my eyes, a specially sinister and

# Vada Frye's Ghosts in the Darkness of Despair

suggestive character. The whole room was, I exactly can't tell how, repulsive to me. There was, I suppose, in its proportions and features, a certain mysterious and indescribable suspicious and apprehensive nature about it that played on the imagination. As I began by saying earlier, nothing, absolutely nothing could have induced me to pass a night alone in it. Still though, there seemed to be something that kept drawing me into the room. I would go in only during the day time and just stand there and look around. Often, while doing so, I would get a cold chill and a sense that I was not alone.

I had not been very long in occupation of the front bedroom, when I began a series of uneasy nights and disturbed sleep. I was usually a sound sleeper, and by no means prone to nightmares. It was however, my destiny, instead of enjoying my customary repose, every midnight to mentally snack on a plate full of horrors. After a preliminary course of disagreeable and frightful dreams, my troubles took a definite form, and the same vision, without an appreciable variation in a single detail, visited me at least every second night in the week.

Now, this dream, nightmare, or infernal illusion-whichever you wish to call it, manifested itself too me as I saw, or thought I saw, with the most abominably clear distinctness, something quiet extraordinary. It was a tableau of horror, which made my nights frightful, and my attention invariably became, I know not why, fixed upon the windows opposite the foot of my bed; and, uniformly with the same effect, a sense of dreadful anticipation always took slow but sure possession of me. I became somehow conscious of a sort of horrid but undefined preparation going forward in some unknown quarter, and by some unknown agency, for my torment; and, after an interval, which always seemed to me of the same length, a picture suddenly floated out of the darkness up to the window, where it remained fixed, as if by an electrical attraction, and my discipline of horror then commenced, to last perhaps for hours. The picture thus mysteriously glued to the window-panes, was the portrait of an old man, in a crimson flowered silk dressing-gown, the folds of which I could now describe, with a countenance embodying a strange mixture of intellect, power, and sinister malignancy. His nose was hooked, like the beak of a vulture; his eyes large, grey, and prominent, and lighted up with a more than mortal cruelty and coldness. These features were surmounted by a crimson velvet cap, the hair that peeped from under it was white with age, while the eyebrows retained their original blackness. I remember today every line, hue and shadow of that stony countenance, and well I should. The gaze of this hellish visage was fixed upon me, and mine returned it with the inexplicable fascination of nightmare, for what appeared to me to be hours of agony. Thus it was every few nights to the point that I often went around days showing exhaustion from lack of sleep. Going to bed at night became a distinct burden on my mind.

Strangely, the visits became less frequent, but did not altogether stop. The evil spirit, who enthralled my senses in the shape of that portrait that appeared in the window, may have been just as near me, just as energetic, just as malignant, though I saw him not except in picture form. Now, I am always in awe of religion and respect it, but never let it interfere with my will to think for myself, which, frankly, bothers many people. I have read the Bible often and know of unclean spirits and demons, but do not believe in such, because I have a mind that must be shown, not massaged into believing that which I cannot see, taste or feel.

One night I was sleeping soundly, when I was roused by a step on the floor outside my room, followed by the loud clang of what turned out to be a large brass flower pot, flung by some force over the stair banisters, and rattling with a rebound down the second flight of stairs; and almost concurrently with this, my door burst open, and a cold wind swirled in.

I had jumped out of bed and just stood there shivering and staring through the doorway at a window at the end of the hall, through which the sickly light of a clouded moon was gleaming through the dark out in the hallway, and I had a feeling that something else was there in the room with me.

Now, I was overwhelmed with fear and I began to think that there was something about that dirty old house that just wasn't right. I sent Riley notice that I would be leaving and returning back to live with my mom and dad. However, he did not want to leave the place empty as it was at the end of the street, and the time, which was 1915, was bad economically, and many times people would squat in vacant houses, sometimes doing great damage. Consequently, he asked me to stay on until he found someone else to live there, or hopefully, found a tenant. I did not tell him the real reason I wanted to leave, as I feared he might think me going insane.

Now, anxious as I was to change my quarters, it so happened, owing to a series of petty procrastinations, all visitations and strange happenings ceased. I was about to conclude that I had simply let my imagination run wild. However, as I was sitting by my bedroom fire, the door being locked for some unknown reason, I heard a step on the flight of stairs descending from the attics. It was two o'clock in the morning, and the streets were as silent as a church yard, and the sounds were, therefore, perfectly distinct. There was a slow, heavy tread, characterized by the emphasis and deliberation of age, descending by the narrow staircase from above; and, what made the sound more singular, it was plain that the feet which produced it were perfectly bare. It was quite plain also that the person who was coming downstairs had no intention whatever of concealing his movements; but, on the contrary, appeared disposed to make even more noise, and proceed more deliberately than was at all necessary. When the step reached the foot of the stairs outside my room, it stopped; and I expected any moment to see my door open spontaneously, and give admission to the original of my detested portrait I had seen in the window. I was, however, relieved in a few seconds by hearing the descent renewed, just in the same manner, upon the staircase leading down to the drawing rooms, and after another pause, I heard no more.

Now, by the time the sound had ceased, I was wound up to a very unpleasant pitch of excitement. I listened, but there was not a stir. I screwed up my courage and opened my door, and in a weak voice said, "Who's there?" There was no answer, as the ringing of my own voice vibrated throughout the house. There is, I think, something most disagreeably disenchanting in the sound of one's own voice under such circumstances, exerted in solitude and in vain. It redoubled my sense of isolation, and as I looked down the hallway, I saw the door to the other bedroom; the one I feared going into at dark, had been left open, and I knew that I always closed it, closed it at the end of the day after going inside as I was prone to do for some unknown reason almost every day, but only during the day, because I felt that there was something in there that might come out at night. I could not bring myself to go down the hallway and close the door. I just couldn't.

So, I went back into my room, closed the door, crawled into bed and like a child, pulled the covers over my head with fright. I somehow drifted off to sleep.

Next night brought no return of my barefooted fellow lodger; but the night following, being in my bed, and in the dark, I suppose, about the same hour as before, I distinctly heard the same thing as someone descended from the attic.

I jumped out of bed, clutched the poker from the fireplace as I passed the expiring fire, and in a moment was upon the hallway. The sound had ceased by this time, and the dark and chill were overwhelming. To my horror, I saw, or thought I saw there in the intense darkness as there was no light and no moon out, a black thing, in the shape of a man shimmering in a mist, standing, with its back to the wall, facing me, with a pair of great greenish eyes shining dimly out. This apparition began to advance upon me.

From an instinct of terror, rather than courage, I hurled the poker its way, with all my force, and in horrid fashion, turned and dashed into my room and double-locked the door. Then, in a minute more, I heard the horrid bare feet walk down the stairs, until the sound ceased, as on the former occasion.

Though they were no longer making noises, in my head I heard those horrid bare feet, and the regular tramp, tramp, tramp, which measured the distance of the entire staircase through the solitude of my haunted dwelling.

Why I stayed, I do not know – pride I suppose, as I did not want to admit to anyone that I was scared of a silly ghost, because I might be ridiculed as childish. I dreaded the approach of the following night. Oh, but it came, ushered ominously in with a thunder-storm and dull torrents of depressing rain. Earlier than usual, the street grew silent, and by twelve o'clock nothing but the comfortless pattering of the rain was to be heard.

I made myself as snug as I could. I kept the light on by my bed. I waited with resolve, for I was determined to face the being, no matter what it was. I was fidgety and nervous and tried in vain to interest myself with a book. I walked up and down my room, whistling music and listening with dread for that horrible noise. I sat down and stared at the door as horrible speculations chased one another through my brain.

Silence, meanwhile, grew more silent, and darkness darker. I listened in vain for the rumble of a vehicle, or the dull clamour of a distant noise. There was nothing but the sound of a rising wind, which had succeeded the thunderstorm. I began to feel myself alone with nature. My courage was ebbing just when I again heard the flabby, naked feet deliberately descending the stairs.

I got up and as I crossed the floor I summoned all my courage. I could hear my on deep breathing as the steps continued. I confess I hesitated for some seconds at the door before I opened it. When I peeped out into the hallway, it was perfectly empty and all sound ceased. I was reassured enough to venture forward nearly to the stairway banisters. Horror of horrors! Within a stair or two beneath the spot where I stood my eye caught something in motion; it was a huge foot, heavy and flapping with a dead weight from one step to another. The thing stared at me – not into my eyes, but my soul. It fixed upon me with an expression of malice; and, as it shuffled about and looked up into my face almost from between my feet, I saw, I could swear that I felt it then, and know it now, the infernal gaze and the accursed countenance of my old friend in the portrait, transfused into the visage of the bloated vermin before me. Yes, it was the man in the portrait.

I raced into my room again with a feeling of loathing and horror I cannot describe, and locked and bolted my door as if the devil, himself, had been at the other side. I eased down onto the floor by the bed shivering with fright and sat and sat and sat until morning.

I decided not to sleep another night in that evil house, but alas, for some reason, I could not bring myself to leave it. Why oh why could I not break free of the place? Now, your granny is not a brave woman, but I am a woman who always faces up to that which I cannot explain. I have no belief in life after death, so I simply could not bring myself to believe that there was a creature roaming about from beyond the grave. I decided it simply had to be my mind playing tricks on me, and for that reason I made a decision I have always regretted.

I determined that I would sleep in the bedroom at the end of the hall – the very room I had

**J. Wayne Frye**

avoided since arriving. So, I was lying in the attitude of sleep, in a lumbering old bed. I hate to think of it. I was really wide awake, though I had put out my light, and was lying as quietly as if I had been asleep; and although accidentally restless, my thoughts were running in a cheerful and agreeable channel.

I think it must have been two o'clock at least when I thought I heard a sound in that odious dark alcove at the far end of the bedroom. It was as if someone was drawing a piece of cord slowly along the floor, lifting it up, and dropping it softly down again in coils. I sat up once or twice in my bed, but could see nothing, so I concluded it must be mice in the walls. I felt no emotion graver than curiosity, and after a few minutes ceased to observe it. However, while lying in this state, strange to say; without at first a suspicion of anything supernatural, all a sudden I saw an old man, rather stout and square, in a sort of black robe moving stiffly and slowly in a diagonal direction, from the alcove, across the floor of the bedroom, passing my bed at the foot, and entering the closet at the left. It was the same man from the portrait. He had something under his arm; his head hung a little at one side, but when I saw his face that awful countenance disclosed what he was. Without turning to the right or left, he passed beside me, and entered the closet by the bed's head. While this fearful and indescribable type of horror was passing, I felt that I had no more power to speak or stir than if I had been myself a corpse.

# Vada Frye's Ghosts in the Darkness of Despair

For hours after it had disappeared, I was too terrified and weak to move. As soon as daylight came, I took courage, and examined the room, and especially the course which the frightful intruder had seemed to take, but there was not a vestige to indicate anybody's having passed there; no sign of any disturbing being whatsoever.

It required some nerve, I can tell you, to go to my haunted chamber next night, and lie down quietly in the same bed. I did so with a degree of trepidation, which, I am not ashamed to say, a very little matter would have sufficed to stimulate to downright panic. This night, however, passed off quietly enough and I grew more confident that it had all been an illusion conjured up by a tired mind affected by an equally tired old house that danced with the creepiness of age.

I tumbled into bed next night, put out my night light, and, went fast asleep. However, I awoke from this deep slumber with a start. I knew I had had a horrible dream; but what it was I could not remember. My heart was thumping furiously; I felt bewildered and feverish; I sat up in the bed and looked about the room. A broad flood of moonlight came in through the window; everything was as I had last seen it except for hearing outside a pleasant little girl apparently singing on her way home, I suppose. Taking advantage of this diversion I lay back down again, with my face towards the fireplace, and closing my eyes, did my best to think of nothing else but the song she was singing. It was *Onward*

**J. Wayne Frye**

# Vada Frye's Ghosts in the Darkness of Despair

*Christian Soldiers,* which was every moment growing fainter in the distance as the singer walked away from the house. And then I heard the distinct sound of what appeared to be a child jumping rope to the cadence of the song. My, it was the child singing, but what was a child doing out so late? I asked myself why I did not also skip away, but knew my curiosity was such that I felt bound to the house.

I sank into a doze, neither sound nor refreshing. Somehow the song had gotten into my head, and I kept repeating it to myself. Suddenly, I sat up and opened my eyes in horror. I saw the same accursed figure standing full front, and gazing at me with its stony and fiendish face. It stood at the foot of my bed. For about three seconds only I saw it plainly; then it grew indistinct; but, for a long time, there was something like a column of dark vapour where it had been standing between me and the wall; and it slowly dissipated.

The next day, I was literally overpowered with fatigue, and longing for sleep as I sat by the fireplace in that infernal bedroom. The window was slightly opened to let in some fresh air, a pleasant freshness pervaded the room, and the cheerful sun of day was making the room quite cherry. What was to prevent my enjoying an hour's nap? The whole air was resonant with the cheerful hum of life, and the broad matter-of-fact light of day filled every corner of the room.

I yielded to temptation, and I lay down, limiting myself to half-an-hour's doze in the luxury of a

# Vada Frye's Ghosts in the Darkness of Despair

soft bed. I lay there in peace, drifting off to sleep. After about half an hour, without a startling episode during sleep, I awoke. Oh, and what I saw right there in the daylight. There was a figure seated in the old sofa-chair, near the fireplace. Its back was towards me, but I could not be mistaken; it turned slowly around, and there was the stony face, glaring at me. There was now no doubt as to its consciousness of my presence, and the hellish malice with which it was animated, for it arose, and drew close to the bedside. There was a rope about its neck, and the other end, coiled up; it held stiffly in its hand. I remained for some seconds transfixed by the gaze of this phantom. He came close to the bed, and appeared on the point of mounting upon it. The next instant I was upon the floor at the far side, and in a moment more was, I don't know how, at the bottom of the stairs. I must have been so frightened I simply did not remember running out of the room. Oh, then I looked up and there came the phantom down the stairs. All this in daylight. Who ever heard of ghosts roaming about in the day?

I stood there at the bottom of the stairs, frozen in fear. The abhorred phantom was before me there; it was standing near the banisters, stooping a little, and with one end of the rope around its neck was making a noose at the other, as if to throw over my neck, so that I might join him in death. While engaged in this baleful pantomime, it wore a smile so unspeakably dreadful, that my senses were nearly overpowered. I collapsed onto the floor and

**J. Wayne Frye**

lost consciousness.

No one can conceive or imagine what it is for flesh and blood to stand in the presence of such a thing, a thing that seems to have come from the very depths of hell. I opened my eyes and a shadow passed over me, sending a chill through my entire body.

For some reason, I felt my horror was over, and I had survived, but I vowed to not tempt fate again. I packed my things furiously and breathed a sigh of relief that I was finally finished with the whole ordeal.

With my suitcase in my hand, I walked down the front steps out into the street, and coming up the lane was the lady who owned the coffee shop. She stopped and asked why I was leaving. I looked at her with piercing eyes and said, "I think you probably know."

I almost sensed a smile on her face as she said, "Of course I do. You see, I know the house's history better than anyone else. My great grandmother is the one who sold it to Judge Hackett. Oh, he was an evil man who would get angry if any child played near the house, disturbing him. Once such little girl was named Emily, and she would be seen going by regularly, skipping rope. Judge Hackett would run and holler at her to move on and play somewhere else."

"One day little Emily was found in the woods behind the house. She was strangled you see, strangled by her skip rope. The culprit was never found, but when all the townsfolk gathered around the poor dead girl's body the judge was heard to whisper under his breath, 'Guess I want have to put up with that infernal skipping rope any more.' And you know at that exact moment, all there claimed to see the girls eyes open, open and stare at the judge."

"Now, the girl's parents, after a few years investigation that led no where, were given the rope and all Emily's other belongings. They took them home, put them in a box and placed the box under her bed."

"About a year later, they made a wild dash to the sheriff's office, proclaiming that someone had gone into that bedroom and apparently stolen the box. That very night, as a man was passing through the alleyway behind this house, he looked up into the back bedroom where the alcove is visible when the lights are turned on and saw a body swaying back and forth, hanging from a rope."

"The sheriff was summoned. He found Judge Hackett hanging in the alcove where he had hanged himself with the very jump rope used by Emily. Oh, and they found the box in the woods right where the body was found, but no rope, of course, as it was around the judge's neck."

I asked the lady if the little girl liked to sing. She said, "Yes, she was always singing *Onward Christian Soldiers*." It was then that I knew what drove the judge to suicide.

# Vada Frye's Ghosts in the Darkness of Despair

## Story 3
## Howard and the Scurrying Blackbirds

*My grandmother was never one to miss the opportunity to tell a good story, and each Christmas, while on a two week vacation from school, I always spent as much time with her as possible, and at night, my grandfather, who went to bed at 7 PM, would leave the two of us alone to contemplate what we might do for entertainment. Sometimes we would play games, and other times we would watch television, especially when Playhouse 90 was on. Playhouse 90 was a show, unlike today's mindless claptrap, that stimulated the mind with stage plays adapted for television. One night, we watched Henry James' ghost story Turn of the Screw on Playhouse 90, and after 90 minutes of terror, I was still not satisfied, so I pleaded with my grandmother to please share a ghost story with me. I had heard many of them often over the years, but this night, she regaled me with a tale she had never shared before.*

# Vada Frye's Ghosts in the Darkness of Despair

Robert Howard awoke suddenly, every nerve tingling with a premonition of imminent peril. He stared about wildly, unable at first to remember where he was, or what he was doing there. Moonlight filtered in through the dusty windows, and the great empty room with its lofty ceiling and gaping black fireplace was spectral and unfamiliar. Then as he emerged from the clinging cobwebs of his recent sleep, he remembered where he was and how he came to be there. He twisted his head and stared at his companion, sleeping on the floor near him. John was but a vaguely bulking shape in the darkness that the moon was shining a gilded light upon.

Howard tried to remember what had awakened him. There was no sound in the house, no sound outside except the mournful hoot of an owl, far away in the piny woods. Now he had captured the illusive memory. It was a dream, a nightmare so filled with dim terror that it had frightened him awake. Recollection flooded back, vividly etching the abominable vision.

Or was it a dream? Certainly it must have been, but it had blended so curiously with recent actual events that it was difficult to know where reality left off and fantasy began.

Dreaming, he had seemed to relive his past few waking hours, in accurate detail. The dream had begun, abruptly, as he and John came in sight of the house where they now lay. They had come rattling and bouncing over the stumpy, uneven old road that led through the pinelands; he and John

# Vada Frye's Ghosts in the Darkness of Despair

wandering far from their North Carolina home, in search of vacation pleasure. They had sighted the old house amidst a wilderness of weeds and bushes, just as the sun was setting behind it. It dominated their fancy, rearing black and stark and gaunt against the low lurid rampart of sunset, barred by the dark pines.

They were tired after bumping and pounding all day over back roads in their quest for the unusual. The old deserted house stimulated their imagination with its suggestion of antebellum splendour and decay. They left the automobile beside the rutty road, and as they went up the winding walk of crumbling bricks, almost lost in the tangle of growth, a flock of blackbirds rose from the trees in a fluttering, feathery crowd and swept away with a low thunder of beating wings.

The place was obviously deserted, so they were tempted to go inside, slowly opening the oak door which sagged on broken hinges. Dust lay thick on the floor of the wide, dim hallway, on the broad steps of the stair that mounted up from the hall. They turned toward a door opposite the landing, and entered a large room, empty, dusty, with cobwebs shining thickly in the corners. Dust lay thick over the ashes in the great fireplace.

They discussed gathering wood and building a fire, but decided against it. As the sun sank, darkness came quickly in the thick blackness of the forest that surrounded them. They knew that rattlesnakes and copperheads haunted Southern forests, and they did not care to go groping for firewood in the dark. They ate frugally from goodies they had in their backpacks, and then rolled in their sleeping bags they had gotten from the car and went instantly to sleep.

This, in part, was what Howard had dreamed. He saw again the gaunt house looming stark against the crimson sunset; saw the flight of the birds as he and John came up the shattered walk. He saw the dim room in which they presently lay, and he saw the two forms that were himself and his companion, lying wrapped in their blankets on the dusty floor. Then from that point his dream altered subtly, passed out of the realm of the commonplace and became tinged with fear. He was looking into a vague, shadowy chamber, lit by the grey light of the moon which streamed in from some obscure source, for there was no window in that room. But in the grey light he saw three silent shapes that hung suspended in a row, and their stillness and their outlines woke chill horror in his soul. There was no sound, no word, but he sensed a presence of fear and lunacy crouching in a dark corner. Abruptly he was back in the dusty, high-ceilinged room, before the great fireplace.

He was lying in his sleeping bag, staring tensely through the dim door and across the shadowy hall, to where a beam of moonlight fell across the stairs, some seven steps up from the landing. And there was something on the stair, a bent, misshapen, shadowy thing that never moved fully into the beam of light. But a dim yellow blur that might have been a face was turned toward him, as

     **J. Wayne Frye**

if something crouched on the stairs, regarding him and his companion. Fright crept through his veins, and it was then that he awoke, if indeed he had been asleep.

He blinked his eyes. The beam of moonlight fell across the stairs just as he had dreamed it did, but no figure lurked there. Yet, his flesh still crawled from the fear the dream or vision had roused in him. His legs felt as if they had been plunged in ice-water. He made an involuntary movement to awaken his companion, when a sudden sound paralyzed him.

It was the sound of whistling on the floor above. It was not carrying any tune, but piping shrill and melodious. Such a sound in a supposedly deserted house was alarming enough; but it was more than the fear of a physical invader that held Howard frozen. He could not himself have defined the horror that gripped him. But John's sleeping bag rustled, and Howard saw he was sitting upright. His figure bulked dimly in the soft darkness, the head turned toward the stairs as evil rose from that weird whistling.

"John," whispered Howard from dry lips. He had meant to shout to tell John that there was somebody upstairs, somebody who could mean them no good; that they must leave the house at once. But his voice died dryly in his throat.

John had risen in a trans-like state. His boots clumped on the floor as he moved toward the door. He stalked leisurely into the hall and slowly and methodically made for the lower landing.

## Vada Frye's Ghosts in the Darkness of Despair

Howard lay incapable of movement, his mind a whirl of bewilderment. Who was that whistling upstairs? Why was John going up those stairs?

The whistling sank to a lower note and died out. Howard heard the stairs creaking under John's measured walking. Now John had reached the hallway above. Suddenly the footfalls halted, and the whole night seemed to hold its breath. Then an awful scream split the stillness, and John started screaming, too.

The strange paralysis that had held Howard was broken. He took a step toward the door, and then checked himself as he heard footsteps coming his way. The footsteps were more deliberate and measured than before. Now the stairs began to creak again. A groping hand, moving along the banister, came into the bar of moonlight; then another, and a ghastly chill went through Howard as he saw that the other hand gripped a hatchet. Was it John who was coming down the stairs, hatchet in hand?

Yes! The figure had moved into the bar of moonlight now, and Howard recognized it. Then he saw John's face, and a shriek burst from Howard's lips. John's face was bloodless, corpse-like; gouts of blood dripped darkly down it; his eyes were glassy and set and blood oozed from the great gash in his forehead.

Howard never remembered exactly how he got out of that accursed house. Afterward he retained a mad, confused impression of smashing his way through a dusty cobwebbed window, of stumbling blindly across the weed-choked lawn, gibbering in frantic horror. He saw the black wall of the pines, and the moon floating in a blood-red mist in which there was neither sanity nor reason.

Some shred of sanity returned to him as he saw the automobile beside the road. In a world gone suddenly mad, that was an object reflecting prosaic reality; but even as he reached for the door, a dry chilling whir sounded in his ears, and he recoiled from the swaying undulating shape that arched up from its scaly coils on the driver's seat and hissed sibilantly at him, darting a forked tongue in the moonlight. It was a snake.

With a sob of horror he turned and fled down the road, as a man runs in a nightmare. He ran without purpose or reason. His numbed brain was incapable of conscious thought. He merely obeyed the blind primitive urge to run until he fell exhausted.

The dark pines flowed endlessly past him; so he was seized with the illusion that he was getting nowhere. But presently a sound penetrated the fog of his terror, the steady, inexorable patter of feet running quickly behind him. Turning his head, he saw something lurking menacingly after him, either wolf or dog he thought, but its eyes glowed like balls of raging, stormy green fire. With a deep gasp he rapidly increased his speed, reeled around a long, winding bend in the road, and heard a horse snort in front of him; saw it rear and heard its rider curse; saw the gleam of metal in the man's lifted right hand.

## Vada Frye's Ghosts in the Darkness of Despair

He staggered and fell, catching at the rider's stirrup as he shouted, "For God's sake, help me! The thing! It killed John. It's coming after me! Look!"

Twin balls of fire gleamed in the fringe of bushes at the turn of the road. The rider swore again, and on the heels of his profanity came the smashing report of his gun again and again. The fire-sparks vanished, and the rider, jerking his stirrup free from Howard's grasp, spurred his horse forward. Howard staggered up, shaking in every limb. The rider was out of sight only a moment; then he came galloping back.

"Took to the brush, wolf maybe, though I never heard of one chasin' a man before. Do you know what it was?"

Howard could only shake his head weakly as the rider, etched in the moonlight, looked down at him, smoking pistol still lifted in his right hand. He was a compactly-built man of medium height, and his broad-brimmed planter's hat and his boots marked him as a rancher or farmer.

"What's all this about, anyway?" The man asked.

"I don't know," Howard answered helplessly. "My name's Howard. John, my friend who was traveling with me, we stopped at a deserted house back down the road to spend the night. Something came out of the darkness and my friend went upstairs and then came back down with a huge gash in his forehead. He had a bloody hatchet in his hand and was walking, but was dead. His head had been split open I tell you. I saw brains and

**J. Wayne Frye**

clotted blood oozing down his face. He was a walking dead man I tell you. John was murdered in that dark upper hallway, and then his dead body came stalking down the stairs with a hatchet in its hand to kill me, I think."

The rider made no reply; he sat on his horse like a statue, outlined against the stars, and Howard could not read his expression, his face shadowed by his hat-brim, as he pleaded with him. "You think I'm mad?"

"I don't know what to think," answered the rider. "It was obviously Benton Manor. My name's Buckner. I live just over by the lake. I am also sheriff of this county – part time, of course, cause county ain't big enough for a full-time sheriff. Heard a lot of noise out this way, so I saddled up my horse and decided to ride over."

He swung off his horse and stood beside Howard, shorter than Howard, but much more muscular. There was a natural manner of decision and certainty about him, and it was easy to believe that he was not a man you messed with.

"Are you afraid to go back to the house?" he asked, and Howard shuddered, but shook his head up and down affirmatively. "I'll go, yes, because I have to check on my friend, but I know he is dead, I mean he was dead, but he was walking I tell you."

"We'll see." The sheriff let go of the reins, hopped off and started filling the empty chambers of his big blue pistol as they walked along together toward the house.

# Vada Frye's Ghosts in the Darkness of Despair

As they made the turn, Howard's blood was ice at the thought of what they might see lumbering up the road with a bloody, grinning death-mask, but they saw only the house looming spectrally among the pines, down the road. A strong shudder shook Howard.

Howard said, "How evil that house looks, against those dark pines! It looked sinister from the very first, when we went up the broken walk and saw those blackbirds fly as we approached."

"Blackbirds," Buckner said as he glanced over at Howard. "You saw the blackbirds?"

"Why, yes! Scores of them perching in the trees adjacent to the house."

They strode on for a moment in silence, before Buckner said abruptly: "I've lived in this county all my life. I've passed the manor place a thousand times, I reckon, at all hours of the day and night. But I never saw a blackbird anywhere around it, or anywhere else in these woods. They ain't common to this area."

"There were scores of them," repeated Howard, bewildered.

"I've seen men who swore they'd seen a flock of blackbirds perched around the house just at sundown," said Buckner slowly. "All black men, except for one old tramp. He was buildin' a fire in the yard, aimin' to camp there that night. I passed along there about dark, and he told me about the birds. I came back by there the next mornin'. The ashes of his fire were there, and his tin cup, and skillet where he'd fried pork, and his blankets

**J. Wayne Frye**

looked like they'd been slept in. Nobody ever saw him again. That was twelve years ago. The blacks say they can see the blackbirds. They say the birds are the souls of the Benton's, let out of hell at sunset. They say the red glare in the west is the light from hell, because then the gates of hell are open, and the Benson's fly out."

"Who were the Benson's?" asked Howard, shivering.

"They owned all this land here. The Civil War ruined them, like it did so many. Some were killed in the war; most of the others died out. Nobody's lived in the manor now for maybe 20, no 25 years, when Miss Elizabeth Benson, the last of the line, fled from the old house one night like it was a plague spot, and never came back to it." He paused for awhile and continued as he stood by the car, "This here your auto?"

"It is, yes," replied Howard as he stared morbidly at the grim house. Its dusty panes were empty and blank; but they did not seem blind to him. It seemed to him that ghastly eyes were fixed hungrily on him through those darkened panes.

The sheriff strode up the broken brick walk matter-of-factly with Howard following close at his heels, his heart pounding rapidly. A scent of decay and mouldering vegetation blew on the faint wind, and Howard grew faint with nausea, that rose from a frantic abhorrence of these black woods and the old plantation house before him that hid forgotten secrets of slavery and bloody pride and mysterious intrigues. He had thought of the South as a sunny, lazy land washed by soft breezes laden with spice and warm blossoms, where life ran tranquilly to the rhythm of people in sunbathed cotton fields, but now he had discovered another, unsuspected side, a dark, brooding, fear-haunted side, and the discovery repelled him.

The oaken door sagged as it had before. The blackness of the interior was intensified by the beam of Buckner's light playing on the sill. That beam sliced through the darkness of the hallway and roved up the stairs, and Howard held his breath, clenching his fists. But no shape of lunacy leered down at them. Buckner went in, walking light as a cat, torch in one hand, gun in the other.

As he swung his light into the room across from the stairway, Howard cried out almost fainting with the intolerable sickness of what he saw. A trail of blood drops led across the floor, crossing the sleeping bag John had occupied, which lay between the door and the one in which Howard had lain. However, Howard's sleeping bag had an occupant. John lay there face down, his cleft head revealed in merciless clarity in the steady light. His outstretched hand still gripped the handle of a hatchet, and the blade was imbedded deep in the blanket and the floor beneath, just where Howard's head had lain when he slept there.

A momentary rush of blackness engulfed Howard. He was not aware that he staggered, or that Buckner caught him as he started to fall forward.

# Vada Frye's Ghosts in the Darkness of Despair

When he could see and hear again, he was held up by Buckner as he became violently sick and hung his head against the nearby mantel, retching miserably. Buckner turned the light full on him, making him blink. Buckner's voice came from behind the blinding radiance, the man himself unseen. "Howard, you've told me a yarn that's hard to believe. I saw something chasin' you, but it might have been a wolf or a mad dog. If you're holdin' back anything, you better spill it. What you told me won't hold in any court. You're bound to be accused of killin' your partner. I'll have to arrest you. If you'll give me the straight goods now, it'll make it easier. Now, didn't you kill this fellow laying here? Wasn't it something like this: you quarrelled, he grabbed a hatchet and swung at you, but you dodged and then let him have it?"

Howard sank down and hid his face in his hands, his head swimming. "I didn't murder John! Why, we've been friends ever since we were children in school together. I've told you the truth. I don't blame you for not believing me. But God help me, it is the truth!"

The light swung back to the gory head again, and Howard closed his eyes as Buckner grunted. "I believe this hatchet in his hand is the one he was killed with. Blood and brains plastered on the blade and hairs stickin' to it - hairs exactly the same color as his. This makes it tough for you, Howard."

"How so?" Howard asked with incredible trepidation.

# Vada Frye's Ghosts in the Darkness of Despair

"Knocks any plea of self-defence in the head. Your friend couldn't have swung at you with this hatchet after you split his skull with it. You must have pulled the axe out of his head, stuck it into the floor and clamped his fingers on it to make it look like he'd attacked you. And it would have been damned clever if you'd used another hatchet."

"But I didn't kill him," groaned Howard. "I have no intention of pleading self-defence."

"That's what puzzles me," Buckner admitted. "What murderer would rig up such a crazy story as you've told me, to prove his innocence? Average killer would have told a logical yarn, at least. Hmmm! Blood drops leadin' from the door. The body was dragged no, couldn't have been dragged. The floor isn't smeared. You must have carried it here, after killin' him in some other place. But in that case, why isn't there any blood on your clothes? Of course you could have changed clothes and washed your hands. But the fellow hasn't been dead long."

"He walked downstairs and across the room," said Howard hopelessly. "He came to kill me. I knew he was coming to kill me when I saw him lurching down the stairs. He struck where I would have been, if I hadn't awakened. That window - I burst out of it. You see it's broken."

"I see. But if he walked then, why isn't he walkin' now?"

"I don't know! I'm too sick to think straight. I've been fearing that he'd rise up from the floor where

**J. Wayne Frye**

he lies and come at me again. When I heard that wolf or whatever it was running up the road after me, I thought it was John chasing me, running through the night with his bloody axe and his bloody head and his death-grin!"

His teeth chattered as he lived that horror over again. Then Buckner let his light play across the floor as he said, "The blood drops lead into the hall. Come on. We'll follow them."

Howard cringed. "They lead upstairs."

Buckner's eyes were fixed hard on him. "Are you afraid to go upstairs, with me?"

Howard replied, "Yes. But I'm going with you or without you. The thing that killed poor John may still be hiding up there."

"Stay behind me," ordered Buckner, almost smiling. "If anything jumps us, I'll take care of it. But for your own sake, I warn you that I shoot quicker than a cat jumps, and I don't often miss. If you've got any ideas of layin' me out from behind, forget them. I want to be fair. I haven't indicted and condemned you in my mind already. If only half of what you're tellin' me is the truth, you've been through a hell of an experience, and I don't want to be too hard on you. But you can see how hard it is for me to believe all you've told me."

Howard wearily motioned for him to lead the way, unspeaking. They went out into the hall, paused at the landing. A thin string of crimson drops, distinct in the thick dust, led up the steps. Howard said, as they ascended the stairs, "One set goin' up, one comin' down. You can see the tracks are bigger than yours. Blood drops all the way, blood on the banisters like a man had laid his bloody hand there, a smear of stuff that looks like brains. So, a dead man, groping with one hand, the other gripping the hatchet that killed him, was walking down the stairs."

"Or, maybe he was carried down," continued the sheriff. "But I have to admit that, if somebody carried him, where are the tracks?"

They came out into the upper hallway, a vast, empty space of dust and shadows where time-crusted windows repelled the moonlight and the ring of Buckner's torch seemed inadequate. Howard trembled like a leaf. Here, in darkness and horror, John had died. With trembling voice, he said, "Somebody whistled up here, and John came, seemingly in a trance as if he were being called."

Buckner's eyes were blazing strangely in the light, kind of smiling. "The footprints on the dusty floor lead down the hall," he muttered. "Same as on the stairs, one set going, one coming."

Behind him Howard stifled a cry, for he had seen what prompted Buckner's exclamation. A few feet from the head of the stairs John's footprints stopped abruptly and then returned, treading almost in the other tracks. And where the trail halted there was a great splash of blood on the dusty floor and other tracks met it, tracks of bare narrow feet. They too receded in a second line from the spot.

Buckner bent over them, swearing. "The tracks meet! And where they meet there's blood and brains on the floor! John must have been killed on that spot with a blow from a hatchet. Bare feet coming out of the darkness to meet shoed feet, then both turned away again; the shoed feet went downstairs, the bare feet went back down the hall." He directed his light down the hall. The footprints faded into darkness, beyond the reach of the beam.

"Suppose your crazy tale was true," Buckner muttered, half to himself. "These aren't your tracks. They look like a woman's. Suppose somebody did whistle, and John went upstairs to investigate. Suppose somebody met him here in the dark and split his head. The signs and tracks would have been, in that case, just as they really are. But if that's so, why isn't John lyin' here where he was killed? Could he have lived long enough to take the hatchet away from whoever killed him, and stagger downstairs with it?"

Howard replied, "I saw him on the stairs. He was dead. No man could live after receiving such a wound."

"I believe it," muttered Buckner. "But it's madness! Or else it's too clever. Yet, what sane man would think up and work out such an elaborate and utterly insane plan to escape punishment for murder, when a simple plea of self-defence would have been so much more effective? No court would recognize that story. Well, let's follow these other tracks." Then, there was that slight smile again, almost as if Buckner was somehow holding something back.

## Vada Frye's Ghosts in the Darkness of Despair

The flashlight slowly faded, and Buckner said, "This has a brand new battery." He turned and continued, "Let's get out of here."

The darkness seemed to engulf them. Buckner retreated, pushing Howard stumbling behind him as he walked backward, pistol cocked and lifted, down the dark hall. In the growing darkness Howard heard what sounded like the opening of a door. And suddenly the blackness about them was vibrant with menace. Howard knew Buckner sensed it as well as the sheriff's hard body was tense and taut.

But without haste he worked his way back down the stairs, Howard preceding him, and fighting the panic that urged him to scream and burst into mad flight. The ghastly thought of a murderer up there brought icy sweat out on his flesh.

They got back downstairs and the flashlight was bright again. Howard said, as he pointed to the room where John's body lay, "Shine the light on John."

Buckner swung the beam around, and Howard was relieved to see the body still there. "I'd go back up," said Buckner, but I am sure the light would fade again and being up there in the dark is not wise. There's no use dodgin' the question. There's somethin' hellish in this house, and I believe I have an inklin' of what it is. I don't believe you killed your friend. Whatever killed him is up there. There's a lot about your yarn that don't sound sane; but there's nothin' sane about a flashlight goin' out like this one did. I don't believe that thing upstairs is human. I never met anything I was afraid to tackle in the dark before, but I'm not goin' up there until daylight."

The stars were already paling when they came out on the broad porch. Buckner seated himself on a broken rocker, facing the door, his pistol dangling in his hand. Howard sat down on the first of three steps that led to the walkway. The two of them sat there all night, just waiting for daylight and Howard lay down in a foetal position and fell asleep. Later, with the morning sun beating down on him, he rose, wincing at the stiffness of his limbs. He looked over at Buckner and said, "I'm ready, let's go."

"I've already been!" Buckner said, his eyes burning in the early dawn. "I didn't wake you up. I went as soon as it was light. I found nothin'."

"The tracks of the bare feet," pleaded Howard.

"Gone," replied Buckner. "Something swept the floor, as all the dust was in the corner, and no footprints."

"What shall we do?" asked Howard. "With those tracks gone, there goes my only chance of proving my innocence."

"Don't worry, I saw them but say nothin' about what's happened here, when we get to town. I'll simply tell the district attorney that John was killed by a party or parties unknown, and that I'm workin' on the case. Are you game to come back with me to this house and spend the night here, sleepin' in that room as you and John slept last night?"

# Vada Frye's Ghosts in the Darkness of Despair

Howard contemplated, and realized he simply was in an untenable position. "He sighed and said, "What choice have I?"

Most of the day was spent with the coroner and county officials, who were frankly, not very professional. The body was removed, and all went back to town. Howard was told to stay until a coroner's inquest could be held. Buckner said he could stay with him, and they went back out to his place and waited for dark, when they got into Buckner's car and drove up the lonely road just as Howard and John had.

Again the shadows were slowly lengthening over the dark pines, and again two men came bumping along the old road. Buckner was driving as Howard's nerves were shattered since the strain of the day added to the horror that still rode his soul like the shadow of a black winged vulture. He had not slept, had not even been able to take but a small bite of food.

"I told you I'd tell you about the Benson's," said Buckner. "They were proud folks and ruthless when they wanted their way. Back in the days of slavery they were known for cruelty to those they owned. The whole family oozed with cruelty, especially one named Celia, the last one of the family to come to these parts when slavery still existed. Even after the Civil War, the slaves were freed, but what could they do but stay on where they had been all their lives for most of 'um. Old man Benson died, and Celia was said to do some type of conjure over his body, and the Blacks still

**J. Wayne Frye**

on the property said the devil was always waitin' for that mean old man out in the pines – just waitin' and was waitin' for Celia, too."

"Well, one by one the blacks left except two or three, cause the land simply wore out and no cotton could be grown. Celia stayed on though, along with her four sisters, growing older and bitterer. They kept to themselves, bein' proud, and ashamed of their poverty. Folks wouldn't see them for months at a time. When they needed supplies they sent one of the former slaves to town after them."

"Miss Celia was exceptionally cruel, got much crueller as time passed. She had a maid from the West Indies, and it was said that she'd beat her really bad, but the maid was so afraid of her that she just took it without complaint. I knew an old timer from way back swore he saw Miss Celia tie this girl up to a tree, stark naked, and whip her with a bullwhip. Nobody was surprised when she disappeared. Everybody figured she'd run away, of course. See, it's 1940 now, so it was about 1895."

"Well, one day in 18 and 99 I believe it was, Elizabeth, the youngest girl, came in to town for the first time in maybe a year. She said the blacks had all left the place. Said Miss Celia had gone, without leaving any word, but she said she thought her sister was there, 'cause there was something strange in the house. She didn't say what she meant. Just got her supplies and went in her horse and buggy back out here. A month went past, and a black came into town and said that Miss

## Vada Frye's Ghosts in the Darkness of Despair

Elizabeth was livin' at the place alone. Said the other two sisters had also gone just like Miss Celia."

"The black man said that Elizabeth was mighty afraid out there, afraid of something terrible. He said he was the last one there with her, and that he wasn't going back. Then, a few months later, just had turned into 1900, Miss Elizabeth came tearin' into town on the one horse she owned, nearly dead from fright. She fell from her horse in the square, and when she could talk she said she'd found a secret room in the place that had been forgotten for years. And she said that there she found her three sisters, dead, and hangin' by their necks from the ceilin'. She said something chased her and nearly brained her with an axe as she ran out the front door, but somehow she got to the horse and got away. She was nearly crazy with fear, and didn't know what it was that chased her, said it looked like a woman with a yellowish face."

"A bunch of men rode out there and searched the house from top to bottom, but they didn't find any secret room, or the remains of the sisters. But they did find a hatchet stickin' in the doorjamb downstairs, with some of Miss Elizabeth's hairs stuck on it, just as she'd said. She wouldn't go back there and show them how to find the secret door; almost went crazy when they suggested it."

"When she was able to travel, the people made up some money and lent it to her and she went to California. She never came back, but later it was learned, when she sent back to repay the money they'd lent her it was learned she'd married out there. Nobody ever bought the house. It stood empty now for nigh onto 50 years."

"So, did people believe her story about what happened?" said Howard.

"Well, most folks thought she'd gone a little crazy, livin' in that old house alone. Some people believed that maid who was beaten so bad by Celia sneaked back there and murdered them all, except Elizabeth, of course.

"Well," interjected Howard. "That woman is long dead. Couldn't be her up there at the top of the stairs."

Buckner wrenched the wheel around and turned into a side road on the right. He said, "Damn, there's an old black man living out on Piney Road who is really old. We need to talk to him. People stay away from him, cause they say he is a practitioner of the black arts – voodoo."

Howard shivered at the phrase, staring uneasily at the green forest walls that shut them in. The scent of the pines was mingled with the odours of unfamiliar plants and blossoms. But underlying all was a reek of rot and decay. Again a sick abhorrence of these dark mysterious woodlands almost overpowered him.

"Here's old Jacob's hut," announced Buckner, bringing the automobile to a halt.

Howard saw a clearing and a small cabin squatting under the shadows of huge trees. A thin wisp of blue smoke curled up from the stick-and-mud chimney. He followed Buckner to the tiny stoop, where the sheriff pushed open the leather-hinged door and walked in. Howard blinked in the comparative dimness of the interior. A single small window let in a little daylight, what little was left that is. An old man crouched beside the hearth, watching a pot stew over the open fire. He looked up as they entered, but did not rise. His face was a mass of wrinkles and his limbs thin and spindly.

Buckner motioned Howard to take a seat, as Buckner took a seat facing the old man. "Jacob" he said bluntly, "the time's come for you to talk after all the years about what you know about that old Benson house. I've never questioned you about it, because it wasn't in my line. But a man was murdered there last night, and this man here may hang for it, unless you tell me what haunts that old house." There was that subdued smile again.

The old man's eyes gleamed, then grew misty as if clouds of extreme age drifted across his brittle mind. "The Bensons" he murmured with a mellow and rich voice. "They was proud people, proud and cruel."

"What of the house?" asked Buckner patiently.

"Miss Celia was the proudest of them all and the cruellest. The black folks hated her, especially the maid, Joan. Miss Celia whipped her brutally."

"What is the secret that house harbours?"

"What secret."

"You know for years that old house has stood there with its mystery. You know something. I know you do."

## Vada Frye's Ghosts in the Darkness of Despair

The old man stirred the stew, and said, "I is not ready to die yet. I talk too much, and I ain't gonna see many more days. You know that, too."

"You mean somebody would kill you if you told me?"

"No human. I be killed by one of them things not human or maybe somebody does they's bidding."

"Exactly what is the non-human thing you fear?"

The old man bowed his head, and seemed to be talking at the floor. "Well, they's a legend 'bout a ancient brew that can do things to people. My mammy had the powers you know – the powers of the black arts. They was this woman came here one time when I was but a boy, just could only see her feet and a little bit of her legs cause I was hiding back in the closet (he pointed to a closet in the far corner). That woman was mean you could tell, filled with evil was she. Told my mammy she'd have her killed if 'un she didn't give her the brew she wanted. The brew was hard to make, but my mammy was afraid of her. So, she got some snake-bones, and the blood of vampire bats, and the dew from an owl's wings, and other elements I can't remember now. Well, this here lady drunk that brew right about where you sittin' now. Told my mammy not to ever tell nobody or she'd kill her for sure. The lady turned around and walked out."

"You telling me what Jacob?"

"I'm telling you that woman walked outta here changed. She weren't no woman no more. She was a creature of the night. She became one who could fetch darkness to blot out what little light they is in this here world. What she became can be slain by only lead or steel, but unless it is slain thus, it lives forever, and it eats no such food as humans eat. It dwells like a bat in a cave or an old house. Time means naught to one of these creatures. It cannot speak human words, nor think as a human thinks, but it can hypnotize the living by the sound of its voice, and when it slays a man it can command his lifeless body until the flesh is cold. As long as the blood flows, the corpse is its slave. Its pleasure lies in the slaughter of human beings. That is what its sustenance is – the lives of human beings."

"And you know not this woman? Was she black or white? At least you could tell that by seeing her legs. Was her name Joan?"

"Joan?" he said slowly. "I have not heard that name for generations. Could a been, but could not a been. You see, I never saw the colour of her skin. She had on high button shoes and a long dress that went to the tops of those shoes."

He reached down to pick up a log to put on the fire, groping among the heaps of sticks there. And his voice broke in a scream, as he jerked back his arm convulsively. And a horrible, thrashing, hissing thing came with the log. It wrapped itself around the man's arm, a hissing rattle snake that bit him furiously again and again. The old man fell on the hearth, screaming, upsetting the simmering pot and scattering the embers, and then Buckner caught up a billet of firewood and crushed the snake. Cursing, he kicked aside the knotting, twisting thing, glaring briefly at the mangled head he had crushed.

Old Jacob had ceased screaming and writhing; he lay still. He lay dead as Buckner said, "That infernal snake crammed enough poison into his veins to kill a dozen men his age. But I think it was the shock and fright that actually killed him."

"What shall we do?" asked Harvey, shivering.

"Leave the body on that bed. Nothin' can hurt it, if we bolt the door so the wild hogs can't get in. We'll carry it into town tomorrow. We've got work to do tonight. Let's get goin'."

Howard said, as they placed the body on the bed, "Something evil did this."

"Ain't no need to get excited. There's nothing supernatural about a snake in these parts. If he'd been a younger man, we could a saved him."

They left with heavy hearts and were turning in to the main road before either spoke again when Howard said, "Joan has been in the house all these years?"

"Well, I am not buying no eternally living creature story, but there is something there alright, but I don't know what."

As they pulled into the long, winding drive the old house was looming black against the red sunset. As they came to a halt, suddenly a huge flock of blackbirds fluttered out of the trees and soared skyward.  .

The oaken door sagged on broken hinges as Buckner opened it. Their feet echoed on the old oaken floor. The blinded windows reflected the sunset in sheets of flickering red flame. As they came into the broad hall, Howard saw the string of black marks that ran across the floor and into the chamber, marking the path of a dead man.

Buckner had brought blankets out of the automobile. He spread them before the fireplace. "I'll lie next to the door" he said. "You lie where you did last night."

Buckner reached into his jacket and brought out an extra gun and handed it to Howard without a word. Howard took it and prowled nervously back and forth, begrudging the slow fading of the light as a miser begrudges the waning of his gold. He leaned with one hand against the mantelpiece, staring down into the dust-covered ashes. The fire that produced those ashes must have been built by one of the Benson's long ago, more than thirty years before. The thought was depressing. Idly he stirred the dusty ashes with his toe. Something came into view among the charred debris, a bit of paper, stained and yellowed. He bent and drew it out of the ashes. It was a notebook with mouldering cardboard backs.

"What have you found?" asked Buckner, squinting down the gleaming barrel of his gun.

"Nothing but an old note-book. Looks like a diary. The pages are covered with writing, but the ink is so faded, and the paper is in such a state of decay that I can't tell much about it. How do you suppose it came in the fireplace, without being burned up?"

# Vada Frye's Ghosts in the Darkness of Despair

"Thrown in long after the fire was out," surmised Buckner. "Probably found and tossed in the fireplace by somebody who was in here stealin' furniture. Likely somebody who couldn't read. There are plenty of folks like that around these parts."

Howard flipped though the crumbling pages listlessly, straining his eyes in the fading light over the yellowed scrawls. Then he stiffened. "Here's an entry that's legible! Listen!" And then he read: *"I know someone is in the house besides me. I can hear someone prowling about at night when the sun has set and the pines are black outside. Often in the night I hear it fumbling at my door. Who is it? Is it one of my sisters? Is it Celia? If it is either of these, why does she steal so subtly about the house? Why does she tug at my door, and glide away when I call to her? Shall I open the door and go out to her? No, no! I dare not! I am afraid. Oh God, what shall I do? I dare not stay here, but where am I to go?"*

"Damn," exclaimed Buckner. "That must be Elizabeth Benson's diary! Go on!"

"I can't make out the rest of the page," answered Howard. "But a few pages further on I can make out some lines." He read again: *"Why did the servants all run away when Celia disappeared? My sisters are dead. I know they are dead. I seem to sense that they died horribly, in fear and agony. But why? Why? If someone murdered Celia, why should that person murder my poor sisters?"* As he finished, there was Buckner's wry smile again.

# Vada Frye's Ghosts in the Darkness of Despair

Bewildered, Howard said, "A piece of the page is torn out. Here's another entry under another date, at least I judge it's a date; I can't make it out for sure."

Then, a look of horror crept across Howard's face. "Oh my, you have to hear this: *"No, no! How can it be? She is dead or gone away. And this, this horror. God, can such things be? I know not what to think. If it is she who roams the house at night, who fumbles at my door, who whistles in the darkness, I must be going mad. If I stay here alone I shall die as hideously as my sisters must have died. Of that I am convinced."*

The incoherent chronicle ended as abruptly as it had begun. Howard was so engrossed in deciphering the scraps that he was not aware that darkness had stolen upon them, hardly aware that Buckner was holding his electric torch for him to read by. Waking from his abstracted state, he darted a quick glance at the black hallway as he said, "What do you make of it?"

"What I've suspected all the time," answered Buckner. "That Celia probably hated the whole family. She is the one old Jacob saw that night when he was in the closet - the one who drank the brew of evil. She's been lurkin' in this old house all these years."

"But why should she murder a stranger?" pleaded Howard.

"You heard what old Jacob said," reminded Buckner, "the satisfaction of evil, nothing else. She mesmerized John, put him in a trance and

86          **J. Wayne Frye**

called him up the stairs, split his head and stuck the hatchet in his hand, and sent him downstairs to murder you. No court will ever believe that though. You are in a pickle my friend."

"She came and peered over the banisters of the stairs at us," muttered Howard. "But why didn't we find her tracks on the stairs?"

"That I cannot answer."

"What am I to do?" pleaded poor Howard.

"I am still trying to figure that out. First, we have to make all things just as they were, and see what happens."

The room needed to be bathed in darkness, so Buckner turned off his flashlight and they both lay down. Howard lay trembling and his heart beat so heavily he felt as if he would suffocate.

Buckner said, "Evidently old Jacob knew what he was talking about, but that doesn't explain the other things, though: the hypnotic powers, the abnormal longevity. That might be your saviour – the longevity. Maybe, just maybe Celia is simply the recipient of some unknown elixir that has prolonged her life. If so, we capture her, or kill the bitch if we must, and you are cleared."

Howard sighed and sat in silence as he heard the pounding of his own heart. Outside in the black woods owls hooted. Then, suddenly the owls stopped and dead silence fell again like a black fog.

Howard forced himself to lie still on his blankets. Time seemed at a standstill. He felt as if he were choking. The suspense was growing unendurable; the effort he made to control his crumbling nerves bathed his limbs in sweat. He clenched his teeth until his jaws ached and almost locked.

He did not know what he was expecting. The fiend would strike again but how and when? Would it be a horrible, sweet whistling, bare feet stealing down the creaking steps, or a sudden hatchet-stroke in the dark? Would it choose him or Buckner? Was Buckner already dead, he actually thought, because he could not see or hear him in the pitch blackness. Ah, he could hear his steady breathing. He thought that Buckner must have nerves of steel. Or was that Buckner breathing beside him, separated by a narrow strip of darkness? Had the fiend already struck in silence, and taken Buckner's place, there to lie in ghoulish glee until it was ready to strike?

He began to feel that he would go mad if he did not leap to his feet, screaming, and burst frenziedly out of that accursed house. Then, just as he was about to get up, the rhythm of Buckner's breathing was suddenly broken, and Howard felt as if a bucket of ice-water had been poured over him. From somewhere above them rose a sound of weird whistling. It was coming!

Howard's control snapped, plunging his brain into darkness deeper than the physical blackness which engulfed him. There was a period of absolute blankness, in which a realization of motion was his first sensation of awakening consciousness. He was running, madly, stumbling over an incredibly rough road. All was darkness about him, and he ran blindly. Vaguely he realized that he must have bolted from the house, and fled for perhaps many kilometres before his overwrought brain began to function. He did not care; dying on the gallows for a murder he never committed did not terrify him half as much as the thought of returning to that house of horror. He was overpowered by the urge to run, run, run blindly, until he reached the end of his endurance. The mist had not yet fully lifted from his brain, but he was aware of a dull wonder that he could not see the stars through the black branches. He wished vaguely that he could see where he was going. He believed he must be climbing a hill, and that was strange, for he knew there were no hills where he was. Then above and ahead of him a dim glow came into focus.

He scrambled toward it, over ledge-like projections that were more and more taking on a disquieting symmetry. Then he was horror-stricken to realize that a sound was impacting on his ears, a weird mocking whistle. The sound swept the mists away. Why, what was this? Where was he? Awakening realization overwhelmed him. He was not fleeing along a road, or climbing a hill; he was ascending some stairs. He was still in the infernal house of evil climbing the stairs to his death.

An inhuman scream burst from his lips. Above it the mad whistling rose in a ghoulish piping of demoniac triumph. He tried to stop, to turn back, even to fling himself over the banisters and tumble below. His shrieking rang unbearably in his own ears. But his will-power was shattered. It did not exist. He had no will. He could not command his own body. His legs, moving stiffly, worked like pieces of a mechanism detached from his brain, obeying an outside will. Clumping methodically, they carried him shrieking up the stairs toward the glowing light that was shimmering now as if signalling him, hypnotizing him.

"Buckner!" he screamed.

His voice strangled in his throat. He had reached the upper landing. He was walking down the hallway. The whistling sank and ceased, but some unknown power still drove him on. He could not see from what source the dim glow came. It seemed to emanate from no central focus. But he saw a vague figure ambling toward him. It looked like a woman, but no human woman ever walked with that skulking gait, and no human woman ever had that face of horror, that leering yellow blur of lunacy. He tried to scream at the sight of that face, at the glint of keen steel in the uplifted claw-like hand, but his tongue was frozen.

Then something crashed deafeningly behind him; the shadows were split by a tongue of flame which lit a hideous figure falling backward. Hard on the heels of the report rang an inhuman squawk.

In the darkness that followed the flash, Howard fell to his knees and covered his face with his hands. He did not hear Buckner's voice as

# Vada Frye's Ghosts in the Darkness of Despair

Buckner's shaking on his shoulder shook him out of his delirium.

A light in his eyes blinded him. He blinked, shaded his eyes, looked up into Buckner's face, Buckner was pale.

"Are you hurt? There's a butcher knife there on the floor."

"I'm not hurt," mumbled Howard. "You fired just in time. Where is it? Where did it go?"

"Listen!"

Somewhere in the house there sounded a sickening flopping and flapping as of something that thrashed and struggled in its death convulsions.

"I hit her, all right. Didn't dare use my flashlight, but there was enough light. When that whistlin' started you almost walked over me gettin' out. I knew you were hypnotized, or whatever it is. I followed you up the stairs. I was right behind you, but crouchin' low so she wouldn't see me, and maybe get away again. I almost waited too long before I fired, but the sight of her almost paralyzed me. Look," he said as he flashed his light down the hallway, and it shone bright and clear on a gaping opening in the wall where no door was before. "It is the secret panel to which Elizabeth alluded," offered Buckner. "Come on!"

He ran across the hallway and Howard followed him dazedly. The flopping and thrashing came from beyond that mysterious opening, and now the sounds had ceased as the light revealed a narrow, tunnel-like corridor that evidently led through one of the thick walls. Buckner plunged into it without hesitation.

"Maybe it couldn't think like a human," he muttered, shining his light ahead of him. "But it had sense enough to erase its tracks last night so we couldn't trail it to that point in the wall and maybe find the secret panel. There's a room ahead. Come with me and finally we will clear up everything once and for all. There is, as they sometimes say, light at the end of the tunnel."

Howard cried out: "It's the place with the three bodies hanging!"

Buckner's light playing about the circular chamber became suddenly motionless. In that wide ring of light three figures appeared, three dried, shrivelled, mummy-like shapes, still clad in the mouldering garments of days gone by. Their slippers were clear of the floor as they hung by their withered skeleton necks from chains suspended from the ceiling.

"The three Benson sisters!" muttered Buckner. "Miss Elizabeth's dream, I mean she said that she sensed her sisters had all been murdered, but the truth will, in the end, be stranger than fiction. Just wait and see." Then his voice became more authoritative as he pointed to the far corner. "There, over there in the corner!"

The light moved, halted and shook in Buckner's hand. "Was that thing a woman once?" whispered Howard. "Look at that grotesque face, even in death. Look at those claw-like hands, with black talons like those of a beast. Yes, it was human, though, even the rags of an old ballroom gown. Why should a maid wear such a dress, I wonder?"

"This has been her lair all these years," muttered Buckner, brooding over the grinning grisly thing sprawled in the corner. "This clears you, a crazy woman with a hatchet, at least 90. That's all the authorities need to know. What evil there is in this place - what evil. She embraced the evil. This is, unfortunately, the way of a world where evil seems to abide. She lowered herself to evil. She loved the evil, sought it out with glee just waiting for someone to enter this old house so she could embrace it, nurture it, bring it out from the darkness." Buckner, almost in a trance-like state now, was grinning as he turned to Howard and said, "But that is not Celia."

"What?"

"No, it is not Celia."

"But look at her. Look. It has to be."

A sinister smile pursed Buckner's lips. "Look, look at her size. Celia was small, only 5:1."

Howard walked a bit closer and looked down at a withered old face. Yes, she was tall. He sighed and said, "But, but…"

"No buts, Howard. You see Elizabeth never left, only pretended to do so and she really was crazy, so crazy that she did not even know she was the killer of her own sisters; she could not break free of this house, ever. She wrote that diary not knowing she was the real killer. She lived a life of delusion, thinking that elixir she got over at Jacob's somehow made her immortal and that she needed human sacrifice to stay alive. The hold of this house was too powerful, and she has used her great nephew all these years to help her in sowing the evil that finally killed her tonight. Her nephew was tired of covering up her murderous rages, but he did enjoy the games he often played with those who somehow managed to escape her wrath initially. It was so much fun, but he had done it for far too long until he simply could go on no more, for he realized that he, too, was going crazy, crazy with the rage that abounds here in this house, and that there was only one way out for him, one way to still his insanity – finally he must kill the old woman to save his own sanity."

Howard stood stunned as Buckner's eyes glossed over. Buckner reached down and picked up the hatchet by his Aunt Elizabeth's side. He raised it high, and the sounds of blackbirds could be heard scurrying from the pines.

## Story 4
## Lovecraft in the Forest of Despair

*My grandmother always said that if you hunted for sport, you were killing for pleasure. She had come up in the country, worked her and her husband's farm for many years, and viewed those who did not eat what they killed as possessing a gene that dated far back in the evolutionary cycle, a gene that made someone seem to relish the sport of killing for pleasure. Now, she was a liberal thinker in a conservative state in a conservative time, but she never wavered in standing up for justice, regardless of the circumstances. She said once "Wayne, I ain't never seen no creature except man that got so much pleasure out of killing. I have killed pigs, chickens, turkeys and the such, but not for pleasure. They were food needed for sustenance. I never enjoyed it, and maybe I should have been a vegetarian, but then again, maybe even plants have feelings. Just don't make no sense to me why there has to be so much killing in*

## Vada Frye's Ghosts in the Darkness of Despair

*this here world.*

*Now, I can relate to the aforementioned Vada Frye philosophy, because she used to tell me story about a hunter who went into the woods and found something very strange. Herewith is another interesting tale that she loving spun to me one Christmas?*

Wingard Lovecraft easily bored and often detached, tired early of hunting for deer illegally out of season. He stood against a sod fence while his host plied, along with some other hunters, toward the thicket beyond in search of game, any game, as they just wanted to kill something. The amusements of life, he assumed, should be accepted with the same philosophy as its ills. It had been a bad day. A heavy rain had made the area so spongy that it fairly sprang beneath the feet. He had come to his friend's estate, primarily because of a woman, newly-minted debutante whom he wanted to meet, but there was also something else more profound. His intimate friend, the companion of his boyhood, the chum of his college days, his fellow-traveller in many lands, the man for whom he possessed stronger affection than any other had mysteriously disappeared with no trace two months ago. He had been a guest on the adjoining estate, shooting with the fervour of the true sportsman, while making eyes, in the intervals, at Adeline Cavan, and apparently in the best of spirits. Miss Cavan blushed whenever he looked at her, and, being one of the best shots in North Carolina, he was never happier than in hunting season. The suicide theory that had been bandied about was preposterous, and there was as little reason to believe him murdered. Nevertheless, he had walked out of the nearby mansion two months ago without hat or overcoat, and had not been seen since. The country was patrolled night and day for over one month. A hundred constables and townsfolk had been beating the woods and poking about, but not so much as a handkerchief had been found. Wingard did not believe for a moment that Wyatt Gifford was dead, and although it was impossible not to be affected by the general uneasiness, he was disposed to be more angry than frightened. At Duke University, Gifford had been an incorrigible practical joker, and by no means had outgrown the habit; it would be like him to cut across the country in his evening clothes, board a cattle-train, and amuse himself by laughing at all his friends out trying to find him. However, Wingard's affection for his friend was too deep to entertain rebuke, and, instead of going to bed early with the other men that night, he determined to walk until ready for sleep. He went down to the river and followed the path through the woods. There was no moon, but the stars sprinkled their cold light upon the pretty belt of water flowing placidly past wood and ruin, between green masses of overhanging rocks or sloping banks tangled with tree and shrub, leaping occasionally over stones. It was very dark in the depths where Wingard trod. He smiled as he recalled a remark of Gifford's: "A forest is like a good many other things in life, very promising at a distance, but a hollow mockery when you get within."

Wingard thought that he could even go farther. The woods need the night to make them seem what they ought to be, what they once were, before people's descendants demanded so much more money for the land they owned, in these greedier days. Wingard strolled along, thinking of his friend, his pranks, many of which had done more credit to his imagination than anything else. Just before the disappearance, they had walked the streets one hot night after a party, discussing the various theories of the soul's destiny. That afternoon they had met at the coffin of a college friend whose mind had been a blank for the past three years. Some months previously they had called at the asylum to see him. His expression had been senile, his face imprinted with the record of debauchery. In death the face was placid, but intelligent. The face was as they had once known it.

Wingard and Gifford had had no time to comment there, and the afternoon and evening were full; but, coming forth from viewing their friend in eternal repose, Gifford had said that the soul sometimes lingers in the body after death. During madness, of course, it is an impotent prisoner, albeit a conscious one. Fancy its agony, and its horror! What more natural than that, when the life-spark goes out, the tortured soul should take possession of the vacant skull and triumph once more for a few hours while old friends gazed upon the person one last time.

Gifford had said, "The body and soul are twins, life comrades, sometimes friends and sometimes enemies, but always loyal in the last instance. Some day, when I am tired of the world, I shall go to a serene mystical place and elevate my consciousness. There are places where they say you can leave your body and go to a higher plain."

The high wild roar of water smote suddenly upon Wingard's ear and checked his memories. He left the forest and walked out on the huge slippery stones by the river wharf at this point, and watched the waters boil down into the narrow pass with their furious untiring energy. The black quiet of the woods rose high on either side. The stars seemed colder and whiter just above.

There was no lonelier spot anywhere he thought than where he was then. All, he surmised, that are here in this wood are me and ghosts, the ghosts of so many from the past who fell prey to this forest of despair. Wingard was not a coward, but he recalled uncomfortably the tales of people who had gone to their deaths in those woods over the years and that many of them swam in the raging river below. Countless people, more venturesome than wise, had gone down into that narrow boiling course, never to appear in the still calm pool beyond, and their bodies were never recovered. Below the great rocks, which formed the walls of a great underground cavern, was believed to be a natural vault, on to whose shelves the dead were drawn. The spot had an ugly fascination. Wingard stood, visioning skeletons, un-coffined and green, the home of the eyeless things which had devoured all that had covered and filled that rattling symbol of man's mortality; then he fell to wondering if any one had attempted to leap into the raging pool of late. It was covered with slime; he had never seen it look so treacherous.

He shuddered and turned away, impelled, despite his bravado, to flee the spot. As he did so, something tossing in the foam below the fall, caught his eye and arrested his retreat. Then, he saw that there was a contrary motion to the rushing water, an upward and backward motion. Wingard stood rigid, breathless; fancying he heard something crackling. Was that a hand? It thrust itself still higher above the boiling foam, turned sidewise, and four frantic fingers were distinctly visible against the black rock beyond.

Wingard's sudden superstitious terror left him. A man was there, struggling to free himself from the suction beneath the whirlpool, swept down, doubtless, but a moment before his arrival, perhaps as he stood with his back to the current. He stepped as close to the edge as he dared. The hand, shaking savagely was clutching, expanding and crying for help as audibly as the human voice. Wingard dashed to the nearest tree, dragged and twisted off a branch with his strong arms, and returned swiftly to the pool. The hand was in the same place, still gesticulating as wildly; the body was undoubtedly caught in the rocks below,

**J. Wayne Frye**

perhaps already half-way along one of those hideous shelves. Wingard let himself down upon a lower rock, braced his shoulder against the mass beside him, then, leaning out over the water, thrust the branch into the hand. The fingers clutched it convulsively. Wingard tugged powerfully, his own feet dragged perilously near the edge. For a moment he produced no impression and then an arm shot above the waters. The blood sprang to Wingard's head; he was choked with the impression that the hand wanted him into the whirlpool. The hand and arm were nearer, although the rest of the body was still concealed by the foam. Wingard peered out with distended eyes. The meagre light revealed the fingers clutching the branch were familiar.

Wingard forgot the slippery stones, the terrible death that waited if he stepped too far. He pulled with passionate will and muscle. Memories flung themselves into the hot light of his brain, trooping rapidly upon each other's heels, as he thought of the drowning person below. Most of the pleasures of his life, good and bad, were identified in some way with his friend, Gifford. Scenes of college days, of travel, where they had deliberately sought adventure and stood between one another and death upon more occasions than one, of hours of delightful companionship among the treasures of art, and others in the pursuit of pleasure, flashed like the changing particles of a kaleidoscope one gazed into as a child with intense fascination and wonderment.

## Vada Frye's Ghosts in the Darkness of Despair

Wingard had loved several women; but he would have flouted in these moments the thought that he had ever loved any woman as he loved Wyatt Gifford. There were so many charming women in the world, and in the thirty-two years of his life he had never known another man to whom he had cared to give his intimate friendship. He threw himself on his face. His wrists were cracking with fatigue; the skin was torn from his hands. Yet, Gifford's fingers still gripped the stick, almost seeming to pull, pull very hard as if he wanted Wingard to fall forward into the swirling water. There was life in those hands yet. Suddenly something gave way. The hand swung about, tearing the branch from Wingard's grasp as it seemed to be trying to pull him in one last time. The body was liberated and flung outward, though still submerged by the foam and spray.

Wingard scrambled to his feet and sprang along the rocks, knowing that the danger from suction was over and that Gifford must be carried straight to the quiet pool. If he survived this, it would not be the first time that his determination had saved him.

As Wingard rushed frantically along the side of the river, he reflected on all the wonderful times he and his friend had over the years. Almost like a man drowning, their life together flashed before him.

Wingard reached the pool. A man in his evening clothes floated on it, his face turned towards a projecting rock over which his arm had fallen,

**J. Wayne Frye**

upholding the body. The hand that had held the branch hung limply over the rock, its white reflection visible in the black water. Wingard plunged into the shallow pool, lifted Gifford in his arms and returned to the bank.

He laid the body down and threw off his coat so he might be free to practice CPR. He was glad of the moment's respite. The valiant life in the man might have been exhausted in that last struggle. He had not dared to look at his face, to put his ear to the heart.

The hesitation lasted but a moment. There was no time to lose. He turned to his prostrate friend. As he did so, something strange and disagreeable hit his senses. For a half-moment he did not appreciate its nature. Then his teeth clenched together and his outstretched arms dropped to his side as there was no need for CPR. He bent down and peered at Gifford. There was no face. It had been furiously nibbled away by fish. The rest of the body was decomposed. Only the hands and part of the arms were whole and seemed alive, but alas, he realized that Gifford had reached for him with dead hands.

As Wingard kneeled there by his friend in disbelief, he realized the forest had claimed Gifford two months before, and Gifford had actually tried to get his friend, his dear friend to join him in death. Tears streamed down his eyes as he realized the love Gifford had for him reached beyond death. He sighed deeply, unable to rise as he closed his eyes for a second. Suddenly his eyes popped open, as he felt two hands grab his neck, strangling the life out of him. As he grasped for breath that would not come, he gazed off in desperation toward the forest where many white spectres were floating their way through the night air. The forest of despair was about to claim another victim with an audience of the dead in attendance.

# Vada Frye's Ghosts in the Darkness of Despair

## Story 5
## Horror With Cold, Icy Fingers

*My grandmother showered me with attention and love. She sensed my loneliness and despair in my search for affection from a father who was generally too busy with the pursuit of wealth to have time for me. She has been gone for many years now, but each day as I lie in bed at night, I reflect on the time we spent together, and all the encouragement she gave me in my literary pursuits. Her storytelling was not only skilfully crafted, but it allowed her to impart that which she had read over the years in a way that titillated a budding mind. She rarely told me where she heard the tales, or what book she read them in. Most times, I assumed she had read them in school or heard them told by her mother, father, relatives or friends. She was a storehouse of knowledge, and each story she spun made me aware of just how important literature (written or oral) is in the flowering of a young mind.*

# Vada Frye's Ghosts in the Darkness of Despair

*What follows is a tale she shared with me many times. In fact, the last time was after she suffered one of many strokes, which made her speech patterns a bit more difficult to follow, but still, she loved sharing stories with me. I was about 20 at the time, and was on Christmas vacation from university. By this time, my grandfather had been dead many years, and as we sat by the pot-bellied stove in her living room reminiscing about my grandfather, I knew she felt somewhat morose about not being able to speak as well. In order to boost her spirits, I decided to ask for a story and with a smile on her face, she shared the following tale.*

Unhappy Wayne is he to whom the memories of childhood bring only fear and sadness. Wretched is he who looks back upon lone hours in vast and dismal misery at time spent longing for some happiness. Such a lot was given to a man named Lovecraft. He lived a life of disappointment and barren misery. And yet he was strangely content, and clung desperately to his sanity, which he often feared losing.

He knew not where he was born, save that it was a vast estate, infinitely old and infinitely horrible; full of dark passages and having high ceilings where the eye could find only cobwebs and shadows. The stones in the crumbling corridors seemed always hideously damp, and there was an accursed smell everywhere, as corpses of the dead were rotting somewhere there abouts. It was never light, so that he used candles to gaze steadily at

**J. Wayne Frye**

dancing shadows on the walls for relief; nor was there any sun outdoors, since the terrible trees grew high above the topmost accessible tower. There was one black tower which reached above the trees into the sky, but that was partly ruined and could not be ascended save by a well-nigh impossible climb up the sheer wall, stone by stone.

He must have lived years in this place, but he lost measure of the time. He thought that someone must have cared for his needs, yet he could not recall any person except himself from his childhood. He thought that whoever reared him must have been shockingly aged, since his first conception of a living person was that of something mockingly like himself, shrivelled and decaying like the castle. To him there was nothing grotesque in the bones and skeletons that were strewn in some of the stone crypts deep down among the foundations.

No teacher urged or guided him, and he did not recall hearing any human voice in all those years, not even his own; for although he knew of speech, he had never thought to try to speak aloud. He remembered there were no mirrors in the castle, and he merely regarded himself by instinct as akin to the youthful figures he saw in books.

Outside, across the putrid moat and under the dark trees, he would often lie and dream for hours about what he read in books; and would longingly picture himself amidst crowds in the sunny world beyond the endless forest. Once he tried to escape from the forest, but as he went farther from the castle the shade grew denser and the air more filled with brooding fear; so he ran frantically back to the castle.

So through endless twilights he dreamed and waited, though he knew not what he waited for. Then in the shadowy solitude his longing for worldliness grew so frantic that he could rest no more, and he decided to scale the ruined tower that reached above the forest into the sky.

In the twilight he climbed the worn and aged stone stairs until he reached the level where they ceased, and thereafter clung perilously to small footholds leading upward. The progress was slow and soon the darkness overhead grew and a chill came over him. As he kept struggling upward, ever upward, he fancied that the end was near.

He felt his head touch a solid thing, and knew he must have gained the roof, or at least some kind of floor. In the darkness he raised his free hand and tested the barrier, finding it stone and immovable. Then came a deadly circling of the tower, clinging to whatever holds the slimy wall could give; until finally his testing hand found the barrier yielding, and he turned upward again, pushing the slab or door with his head as he used both hands in his farther ascent. There was no light revealed above, and as his hands went higher he knew that his climb was for naught; since the slab was the trap-door of an aperture leading to a level stone surface of greater circumference than the lower tower, no doubt the floor of some lofty observation chamber. He slowly crawled through carefully and tried to prevent the heavy slab from falling back into place; but failed in the latter attempt. As he lay exhausted on the stone floor he heard the eerie echoes of its fall, but hoped when necessary to pry it open again.

Believing he was above the trees in the forest, he dragged himself up from the floor and fumbled about for windows so that he might look upon the sky, the moon and stars. However, he was disappointed when all he found were vast shelves of marble, bearing oblong boxes of disturbing size. He saw a huge stone door and pried it open. He walked into a huge room with grated iron railings and was thrilled to bathe in the radiant full moon, which he had never observed before living in the darkness of the castle where he had been shut off from the outside world, except for that one time in the forest which only lasted a short while.

Fancying now that he had attained the very pinnacle of the castle, he commenced to rush up the few steps beyond the door; but the sudden veiling of the moon by a cloud caused him to stumble, and he felt his way more slowly in the dark. It was still very dark when he reached the top grating and found it unlocked, but which he did not open for fear of falling from the amazing height to which he had climbed. Then the moon came out again.

Suddenly he was gripped with terror at the bizarre marvels before him. The sight itself was as simple as it was stupefying, for instead of a dizzying prospect of treetops seen from a lofty perch, there stretched around him a seemingly new world as a great panorama opened before him. He observed an ancient looking stone church, with a soaring spire gleaming in the moonlight.

Half unconscious, he opened the grating and staggered out upon the white gravel path that stretched away in two directions. His mind, stunned and chaotic as it was, still held the frantic craving for light; and not even the fantastic wonder which had happened could stay his course. He neither knew nor cared whether his experience was insanity, dreaming, or magic; but was determined to gaze on brilliance and gaiety at any cost. He knew not who he was or what he was, or what his surroundings might be; though as he continued to stumble along he became conscious of a kind of fearsome latent memory that made his progress not wholly fortuitous. He passed under an arch out of that region of slabs and columns, and wandered through the open country; sometimes following the visible road, but sometimes leaving it curiously to tread across meadows where only occasional ruins bespoke the ancient presence of a forgotten road. He treaded across a shallow river where crumbling, mossy masonry told of a bridge long vanished.

Over two hours must have passed before he reached what seemed to be his goal, a venerable ivied castle in a thickly wooded park; maddeningly familiar, yet full of perplexing strangeness. He saw that the moat was filled in, and that some of the towers were demolished. What he observed with chief interest and delight were the open windows, gorgeously ablaze with light and sending forth sounds of the gaiety within. Advancing to one of these, he looked in and saw an oddly dressed company speaking to one another. He had never, seemingly, heard human speech before; and could guess only vaguely what was said. Some of the faces seemed to hold expressions that brought up incredibly remote recollections; others were utterly alien.

He stepped through the low window into the brilliantly lighted room. The nightmare was quick to come; for as he entered, there occurred immediately one of the most terrifying demonstrations he had ever conceived. Scarcely had he crossed the sill when there descended upon the whole company a sudden and unheralded fear of hideous intensity, distorting every face and evoking the most horrible screams from nearly every throat. Flight was universal, and in the clamour and panic several fell in a swoon and were dragged away by their madly fleeing companions. Many covered their eyes with their hands, and plunged blindly and awkwardly in their race to escape; overturning furniture and stumbling against the walls before they managed to reach one of the many doors.

The cries were shocking; and as he stood in the brilliant room alone and dazed, listening to their vanishing echoes, he trembled at the thought of what might be lurking near him unseen. At a casual inspection the room seemed deserted, but when he moved toward one of the alcoves he detected a presence there, a hint of motion beyond the golden-arched doorway leading to another and somewhat similar room. As he approached the arch he began to perceive the presence more clearly; and then, with the first and last sound he ever uttered, he beheld in full, frightful vividness the indescribable monstrosity which had by its simple appearance changed a merry company to a herd of delirious fugitives.

It was a compound of all that is unclean, uncanny, unwelcome, abnormal, and detestable. It was the ghoulish shade of decay, antiquity, and desolation; the putrid, dripping unwholesome revelation; the awful baring of that which the merciful earth should always hide. It was not of this world, or no longer of this world, yet to his horror he saw in its eaten-away and bone-revealing outlines a leering, abhorrent travesty on the human shape; and in its mouldy, disintegrating apparel an unspeakable quality that chilled him.

He was almost paralyzed, but not too much so to make a feeble effort toward flight; a backward stumble which failed to break the spell in which the nameless, voiceless monster held him. His eyes, bewitched by the glassy orbs which stared loathsomely at him, refused to close; though they were mercifully blurred. He tried to raise his hand to shut out the sight, yet so stunned were his nerves that his arm could not fully obey his will. The attempt, however, was enough to disturb his balance; so that he had to stagger forward several steps to avoid falling. Nearly mad, he found himself yet able to throw out a hand to ward off the apparition which pressed so very menacingly close to him ; when in one cataclysmic second of his nightmare his fingers touched the rotting outstretched paw of the monster beneath the golden arch.

He did not shriek, but all the fiendish ghouls that ride the night-wind shrieked for him as in that same second there crashed down upon his reeling mind a single and fleeting avalanche of soul-annihilating memory. He knew in that second all that had been; he remembered beyond the frightful castle and the trees, and recognized the altered edifice in which he now stood; he recognized, most terrible of all, the unholy abomination that stood leering before him as he withdrew his sullied fingers.

In the supreme horror of that second he forgot what had horrified him, and the burst of black memory vanished in a chaos of echoing images. In a dream he fled from that haunted and accursed pile, and ran swiftly and silently in the moonlight. When he returned to the churchyard place of marble and went down the steps he found the stone trap-door immovable; but he was not sorry, for he had hated the antique castle and the trees. Now he rode with the mocking and friendly ghouls on the night-wind for he knew that light was not for him, nor any gaiety. Yes, he now knew the truth.

## Vada Frye's Ghosts in the Darkness of Despair

Although he was calmed now, he knew why he was shielded from humanity. Why he was alone and no one would talk to him. Why no one saw him or heard him. He knew what that abomination was that he saw, and touched, feeling its cold deadness. Yes, what he had touched after all in that room had fled in fear was a cold and unyielding surface of polished glass called a mirror. Oh my, he was dead!

J. Wayne Frye

## Story 6
## Julius Long – Death Comes Calling

*My grandmother was an uneducated woman, but she was a fervent reader. I recall many books lying about and detective magazines gracing tables about her modest home. Her formal education was limited, but her thirst for knowledge was unlimited, which is why her repertoire of tales was so voluminous. What she read, she retained, and though sometimes using inarticulate language, she could regale you with passion when relating a story. I especially enjoyed her rendition of Room 212, shared with her by Julius Long.*

As a young girl, I lived for awhile in an Asheboro hotel, as in those days hotels were more modestly priced and would give you a weekly or monthly rate that was often cheaper than renting an apartment. Thus I took up residence in the Holmes Hotel, the one on Main Street, which now sits abandoned.

## Vada Frye's Ghosts in the Darkness of Despair

I and a very old lady were two of the three long-term residents, the other person being a man in number 212. I did not even know his name. He never patronized the hotel restaurant, and he did not use the lobby. On the three occasions when we passed each other by, we did not speak, although we nodded in a semi-cordial, noncommittal way. I wanted very much to make his acquaintance. It was lonesome in the dreary hotel. **With the exception of the aged lady down the corridor,** the only permanent guests, as I said, were the man in number 212 and myself. However, I did enjoy the quiet there.

I constantly wondered about the man in 212. He was very pale. Yet I could not believe that he was ill, for his paleness was not of a sickly cast, but rather wholesome in its clarity. His carriage was that of a man enjoying the best of health. He was tall and ram-rod straight. He walked erectly and with a brisk, athletic stride. His pallor was no doubt congenital, not a result of illness.

He must have traveled there by auto, for he certainly was not a passenger on the train that brought me up from Denton, and he checked in only a short time after my arrival. I had briefly rested in my room and was walking down the stairs when I encountered him ascending with his bag. It is odd that our venerable bell-boy did not show him to his room.

It is odd, too, that, with so many vacant rooms in the hotel, he should have chosen 212 at the extreme rear. The building is, as you know

## Vada Frye's Ghosts in the Darkness of Despair

Wayne, a long, narrow affair three stories high. The rooms were all on the east side, as the west wall was flush with a decrepit business building. The corridor was long and drab, and its stiff, bloated paper exuded a musty, unpleasant odour. The feeble electric bulbs that lit it shone dimly as from a tomb. Revolted by this corridor, I insisted vigorously upon being given number 201, which was at the front and blessed with southern exposure. The room clerk, a disagreeable fellow with a Hitler moustache, was very reluctant to let me have it, as it is ordinarily reserved for his more profitable transient trade, but you know how stubborn your grandmother can be.

I had been there exactly a week, and although there are many good people in Asheboro, I sensed that some people were part of a stratified social order where strangers, unless part of the elite, were not easily integrated into the society. Of course, my courtesy toward the Negroes also set me apart, as you know Wayne how southern culture was always adamant back then about the separation of the races. In fact, I was told by one man in the hotel lobby that I should not fraternize with the coloured help, as I was prone to do on occasion. Of course, that is a separate issue that I shall, perhaps, cover in another future story.

Despite the sometimes coolness of my reception, I had never given up hope of making more friends. In the back of my mind I cherished hopes that I might encounter the pale man in 212. However, for some reason, he moved from 212 to 211. There was certainly little advantage in coming only one room nearer to the front. Strange, I thought.

The day after he moved, we nodded to each other again, and this time I thought I detected a certain satisfaction in his sombre, black eyes. He must have known that I was eager to make his acquaintance, yet his manner forbid such overtures. I have never been the sort to run after anybody. Still, the man was an enigma to me.

I began to reflect on his nature and wondered where the pale man took his meals. I had been absenting myself from the hotel restaurant and patronizing the restaurants outside but never saw him at any of them.

Obviously, I thought that he must be difficult to please as he changed rooms again. This time he moved to room 210. I used his inability to locate himself permanently as an excuse for starting a conversation. I said to him in the hallway, "I see we are closer neighbours now." All he did was smile cordially and nod his head.

Next day, he did it again. He moved to room 209. I became intrigued by his little game. What possible motive could he have? I began to contemplate his next move, because I knew the lady in 208 had told me she would be there for a week.

Well, the mysterious guest was not forced to remain where he was, nor did he have to skip a room. The lady in number 208 simplified matters by conveniently dying in her sleep. No one knew the cause of her death, but it was generally attributed to old age. She was buried the same day as her death in potter's field. I was among the curious few who attended her funeral. When I returned home from the mortuary, I was in time to see the pale man going into her room. Already he had moved in.

He favoured me with a smile whose meaning I tried in vain to decipher. Yet, he acted as if there were between us some secret that I failed to appreciate. Alas, then he moved to 207. I would have been astonished if he had not made his scheduled move. I almost gave up trying to understand his eccentric conduct. There was something indefinably unusual about his manner. I became terribly curious to hear his voice. I postulated that he might be a foreigner who spoke no English.

The next day I became very worried. I awoke to find myself lying prone upon the floor. I was fully clothed. I must have fallen exhausted there after I returned to my room the previous night. Still, my concern for what happened diminished when the pale man did an astounding thing. He skipped three rooms and moved all the way to number 203. We were now very close neighbours.

I became ill though and confined myself to my bed for a few days, even having my food brought to me. I even called a local doctor, whom I suspected to be a quack. He looked me over with professional indifference and told me not to leave my room. For some reason, he did not want me to climb stairs. For this bit of information he received a ten-dollar bill which, as I directed him, he fished out of my coat pocket. A pickpocket could not have done it better.

The pale man was still up to his old tricks. When I tottered down the hall, the door of number 202 was ajar. Without thinking, I looked inside. The pale man sat in a rocking-chair idly staring off into space. He looked up into my eyes and smiled that peculiar, ambiguous smile that deeply puzzled me. I moved on down the corridor, not so much mystified as annoyed. The whole mystery of the man's conduct was beginning to irk me, to bother me immensely.

I felt that I would never formally meet the pale man. But, at least, I was going to learn his identity as I determined I would ask the desk clerk about him. Still bed ridden, I summoned the desk clerk to my room and asked point blank who the man in 202 was.

The clerk, looking confused, said, "You must be mistaken. That room is unoccupied."

"Oh, but it is," I snapped in irritation. "I saw the man there only two nights ago. He is a tall, unusual fellow with dark eyes and hair. He is unusually pale. He checked in the day that I arrived."

The hotel man regarded me dubiously, as if I were trying to impose upon him. He said, "But I assure you there is no such person in the hotel. As for his checking in when you did, you were the only guest we registered that particular day.

# Vada Frye's Ghosts in the Darkness of Despair

"What?" I replied. "Why, I've seen him twenty times! First he had 212 at the end of the corridor. Then he kept moving toward the front. Now he's next door in 202."

The room clerk threw up his hands and said, "You're crazy!"

I shut up at once and dismissed him. After he had gone, I heard him rattling the knob of the pale man's door. There was no doubt that he believed the room to be empty, and he certainly believed me to be crazy.

Thus it was that I could then understand the events of the past few weeks. I comprehended the significance of the death in number 207. I even felt myself partly responsible for the old lady's passing. After all, I brought the pale man with me. But it was not I who fixed his path. Why he chose to approach me room after room through the length of this dreary hotel, why his path crossed the threshold of the woman in number 207, those mysteries I could not explain.

I supposed I should have guessed his identity when he skipped the three rooms the night I fell unconscious upon the floor. In a single night of triumph he advanced until he was almost to my door. Yes, he was coming for me, and I knew why he was pale.

He was coming slowly for me. If he had carried a scythe in his hand I would have more easily recognized him. I decided that, regardless of my condition, I was checking out. I packed my bags and literally ran from the hotel.

## Vada Frye's Ghosts in the Darkness of Despair

On the street, I passed a man in a cloak that covered his head. I heard him ask another person on the street, if he knew a man named Julius Long. The next morning, when I read the paper and saw that a Julius Long had died the previous day, I knew the truth, I knew that the pale man would always be looking for me, but you see, that was no man. That was death come calling!

**J. Wayne Frye**

# Vada Frye's Ghosts in the Darkness of Despair

## Story 7
## William Hodgson's Demise

*I was lucky to have two grandparents who were beyond the pale of manipulation in a society where conformity is the norm. Question authority, refuse to follow the prescribed course as dictated by those in control, and you are branded a miscreant and unpatriotic to the ideals of America.*

*My own father was a product of that same will my grandparents instilled in me not to allow others to do your thinking for you. It is a sometimes lonely road for those of us who rebel against convention and conformity, but it is a road I travel with assuredness that I shall not bend before the injustice of the stern manipulators who hurl vindictive tirades of discontent that labels all those who reject the narrow path of hypocrisy that is laid out in a world that has long ago lost its way to compassion and understanding. Christmas time was more than just tales of the macabre, as many*

# Vada Frye's Ghosts in the Darkness of Despair

*of the ghostly renditions my grandmother wove, sowed an intricate tapestry of mental stimulation.*

*One of the most provoking tales she shared at Christmas time occurred in my twentieth year, as her own time was drawing to a close. Little did I know at the time that each tale she shared would lie dormant for so many years, until I would resurrect them here for posterity. She was born in 1899, so she saw and heard things that seemed foreign to me and even more foreign to my progeny. She could recall sailing vessels with great sheets of canvas that used wind to propel them. She knew horse and buggies as chief modes of transportation. She recalled families sharing time rather than being glued to the banal entertainment on television. She was born at the turn of the 20th century when crass materialism had not destroyed compassion. Oh, and how she could spin those grand tales of the macabre.*

It was a dark, starless night. A group of men were becalmed in the northern Pacific. Their exact position William Hodgson did not know; for the sun had been hidden during the course of a weary, breathless week by a thin haze which had seemed to float above him and the others about the height of the mastheads, sometimes descending and shrouding the surrounding sea.

With there being no wind, they had steadied the tiller, and he was the only man on deck. The crew, consisting of two men and a boy, were sleeping forward in their cabins, while Will, his friend, and the master of the little craft, was aft in his bunk on

**J. Wayne Frye**

the port side of the open cabin. The sails were silent as no breeze was about to fill them. Suddenly, from out of the surrounding darkness, there came a voice. "Ship ahoy."

The cry was so unexpected that William gave no immediate answer, because of surprise. Then, it came again, a voice curiously throaty and inhuman, calling from somewhere upon the dark sea away on the portside. "Ship ahoy."

"Hello! William sang out, having gathered his wits somewhat. "Where are you, mate? What do you want?"

"You need not be afraid," answered the queer voice, having probably noticed some trace of timidity in William's tone. "I am friendly."

The response sounded odd, but it was only afterward that it came back to William with any significance. "Why don't you come alongside, then?" he queried somewhat snappishly.

"I can't. It wouldn't be safe. I, I, I." The voice broke off, and there was deathly silence.

"What do you mean?" William asked. "What's not safe? Where are you?"

There came no answer. And then, William stepped swiftly to the side and took out the lighted lamp. At the same time, he knocked on the deck with his heel to waken Will. Then he was back at the side, throwing the funnel of light out into the silent immensity beyond the rail. As he did so, he heard a slight muffled cry, and then the sound of a splash, as though someone had dipped oars into the water.

## Vada Frye's Ghosts in the Darkness of Despair

"Hello, there!" William called again and again as nothing but silence replied. Then, within that silence he could hear the indistinct sounds of a boat being pulled away into the night.

Will came on deck and asked what was up, and William motioned for him to come over to him, which he did with sleepiness still half closing his eyes. "What is it?" he asked, coming across the deck. William related what had happened. He put several questions; then, after a moment's silence, he raised his hands to his lips and shouted, "Ahoy!"

From a long distance away there came back to them a faint reply, William repeated his call. Presently, after a short period of silence, there grew the muffled sound of oars, at which William hailed again.

This time there was a reply: "Put away the light."

"I'm damned if I will," William muttered; but Will told him to do as the voice asked, and he shoved it down under the bulkhead.

"Come nearer," Will said, and the oar strokes continued. Then, they again ceased.

"Come alongside!" exclaimed William. "There's nothing to be frightened of aboard here."

"Promise that you will not show the light?"

"What's wrong with an infernal light?" William shouted?

"Because...." began the voice, and stopped short.

"Because what?" William asked quickly.

**J. Wayne Frye**

# Vada Frye's Ghosts in the Darkness of Despair

Will put his hand on William's shoulder and whispered, "Let me talk to him."

He leaned over the rail. "See here, mister," he said, "this is a pretty queer business, you coming upon us like this, right out in the middle of the blessed Pacific. How are we to know what sort of trick you're up to? You say there's only one of you. How are we to know, unless we get a look at you? What's your objection to the light, anyway?"

As he finished, William heard the noise of the oars again, and then the voice came, but now from a greater distance and sounding extremely hopeless and pathetic. "I am sorry, sorry! I would not have troubled you, only I am hungry, and so is she."

The voice died away, and the sound of the oars, dipping irregularly, was borne to the two men.

"Stop!" sang out Will. "I don't want to drive you away. Come back! We'll keep the light hidden if you don't like it."

"Won't you come alongside now?" asked Will in a shaky voice. "We will not shine the light on you."

"I cannot come closer," replied the voice, and then almost pleading said, "water and food are desperately needed."

"The lady is she OK?" said Will abruptly.

"I have left her behind on the island," came the reply.

"What island?" William cut in.

"I do not know its name," returned the shaky voice.

# Vada Frye's Ghosts in the Darkness of Despair

"Could we not send a boat for her?" asked Will almost desperately.

"No!" said the voice, with determined emphasis. "Absolutely not!" There was a moment's pause; then the voice added, in a tone which seemed a reproach, "It was because of our want I ventured, because her agony tortured me."

"OK!" exclaimed Will. "Just wait a minute, whoever you are, and I will bring you up something at once."

In a couple of minutes he was back again, and his arms were full of various edibles. He paused at the rail. "Can't you come alongside for them?" he asked.

"No, I dare not," replied the voice, and it seemed to William that in its tones he detected a note of craving, as though the owner hushed a mortal desire. It came to him then in a flash that the poor old creature out there in the darkness was suffering for actual need for that which Will held in his arms; and yet, because of some unintelligible dread, refraining from dashing to the side of the schooner and receiving it. And with lightning like conviction there came the knowledge that the invisible person was not mad, but sanely facing some intolerable horror that was on that island.

William said to Will, "Get a box. We must float off the stuff to him in it."

This they did, propelling it away from the vessel, out into the darkness, by means of a boat hook. In a minute a slight cry from the invisible

**J. Wayne Frye**

person came to them, and they knew that he had secured the box.

A little later the person called out a farewell to them. Then, they heard the ply of oars across the darkness.

William turned to Will and said, "I think somehow he'll come back."

"And the lady," said Will. For a moment he was silent; then he continued, "It's the queerest thing ever I've tumbled across since I've been on the sea."

"Yes," William said and fell to pondering the situation.

And so the time slipped away, an hour, another, and still Will stayed on deck; for the queer adventure had knocked all desire for sleep out of him. The third hour was three parts through when they heard again the sound of oars across the silent ocean. The dipping of the oars grew nearer, and William noted that the strokes were firmer and longer. The food had been needed. They came to a stop a little distance off the broadside, and the queer voice came again to them through the darkness: "Schooner, ahoy!"

"That you?" asked Will.

"Yes," replied the voice. "I left you suddenly, but there was great need."

"The lady?" questioned Will.

"The lady is grateful. She will be more grateful soon in the after-life."

Will began to make some reply, in a puzzled voice, but became confused and broke off.

William said nothing as they contemplated what the voice had conveyed.

"I thank you for your kind charity this night," said the voice. "Be sure that it has not escaped his notice."

The voice stopped, and there was a full minute's silence. Then it came again. "We have spoken together upon that which has befallen us. We had thought to go out, without telling anyone of the terror which has come into our lives. She is with me in believing that tonight's happenings are under a special ruling, and that we should tell to you all that we have suffered since."

"Since what?" said Will softly.

"Since the sinking of the Albatross."

"Ah!" William exclaimed. "She left Yokahama some six months ago, and hasn't been heard of since."

"Yes" answered the voice. "But some few degrees to the north of the line, she was caught in a terrible storm. When the calm came, it was found that she was leaking badly, and presently, it falling to a calm, the sailors took to the boats, leaving a young lady, my fiancée, and myself upon the wreck.

"We were below, gathering together a few of our belongings, when they left. They were entirely callous, through fear, and when we came up upon the decks, we saw them only as small shapes afar off upon the horizon. Yet we did not despair, but set to work and constructed a small raft. Upon this we put such few stores as it would hold, including a quantity of water and some ship's biscuits. Then, the vessel, being very deep in the water, we got ourselves onto the raft and pushed off. It was later that I observed we seemed to be in the way of some tide or current, which bore us from the ship at an angle, so that in the course of a few hours the ship became invisible to our sight. Then, toward evening, it grew misty, and for five days we drifted through this strange haze, until, within a few days, we found that we were in a sort of great lagoon, but of this we noticed little at the time; for close before us, through the enshrouding mist, loomed the hull of a large sailing vessel and we thought that was an end to our perils. It wasn't."

"The raft drew near to the ship, and we shouted on them to take us aboard; but none answered. Presently the raft touched against the side of the vessel, and seeing a rope hanging downward, I seized it and began to climb. Yet I had trouble getting up the rope, because there was a slippery grey fungus on it.

"I reached the rail and clambered over it, onto the deck. Here I saw that the decks were covered in great patches with the grey mass, some of them rising into nodules several feet in height; but at the time I thought less of this matter than of the possibility of there being people aboard the ship. I shouted, but none answered. Then I went to the door below. I opened it and peered in. There was a great smell of staleness, so that I knew in a moment that nothing living was within, and with the knowledge, I shut the door quickly, for I felt suddenly afraid."

"I went back to the side where I had scrambled up. My sweetheart was still sitting quietly upon the raft. Seeing me look down, she called up to know whether there were any aboard the ship. I replied that the vessel had the appearance of having been long deserted, but that if she would wait a little, I would see whether there was anything in the shape of a ladder by which she could ascend to the deck. Then we would make a search through the vessel together. A little later, on the opposite side of the decks, I found a rope side ladder. This I carried across, and a minute afterward she was beside me."

"Together we explored the ship, but nowhere was there any sign of life. Here and there, within the cabins themselves, we came across odd patches of that fungus; but this, as my sweetheart said, could be cleansed away. In the end, having assured ourselves that the after portion of the vessel was empty, we picked our ways to the bow, between the ugly grey nodules of that strange growth; and here we made a further search, which told us that there was indeed none aboard but ourselves. Together we cleared out and cleaned two of the cabins, and after that I made an examination whether there was anything eatable in the ship. This I soon found was so. In addition to this I discovered a fresh-water pump, and having fixed it, I found the water drinkable, though somewhat unpleasant to the taste. For several days we stayed aboard the ship without attempting to get to the shore. We were busily engaged in making the place habitable. Yet, we became aware that our lot was even less to be desired than might have been imagined; for though, as a first step, we scraped away the odd patches of growth that studded the floors and walls of the cabins with fervour, they returned almost to their original size within the space of twenty-four hours, which not only discouraged us but gave us a feeling of vague unease. One morning, my sweetheart woke to find a small patch of the slime growing on her pillow, close to her face. It was then we immediately decided to get ashore."

"Hurriedly we gathered together our few belongings, and even among these I found that the fungus had been at work, for one of her shawls had a little lump of it growing near one edge. I threw the whole thing over the side without saying anything to her. The raft was still alongside, but it was too clumsy to guide, and I lowered down a small boat that hung across the stern, and in this we made our way to the shore. Yet as we drew near to it, I became gradually aware that here the vile fungus, which had driven us from the ship, was growing. Here and there it took on the forms of vast fingers, and in others it just spread out flat and smooth and treacherous. Odd places, it appeared as grotesque stunted trees, extraordinarily kinked and gnarled. At first it seemed to us that there was no single portion of the surrounding shore which was not hidden beneath the masses of the hideous slimy plants; yet in this I found we were mistaken, for somewhat later, coasting along the shore at a little distance, we found a smooth white patch of what appeared to be fine sand, and there we landed. It was not sand. What it was I do not know. All that I have observed is that upon this one sandy looking area the fungus will not grow.

"We settled in on this seemingly safe shore, going back to the ship for such things as it seemed to us we should need. Among other matters, I managed to bring ashore with me one of the ship's sails which I used to make small tents. We were happy for awhile, but then it was on the thumb of her right hand that the growth first showed. It was only a small circular spot, much like a little grey mole. We cleansed it, between us, constantly washing it. In the morning of the following day she showed her hand to me again. The grey warty thing had returned. For a little while we looked at one another in silence. Then, still wordless, we started again to remove it. In the midst of the operation she noticed something on the side of my face. My finger rested upon the place, and then I knew and we were, all at once, afraid of something worse than death. We spoke of loading the boat with provisions and water and making our way out onto the sea; yet we were helpless, for many causes, and the growth had attacked us already. We decided to stay, so as not to spread this infernal evil. A month, two months, three months passed and the places grew somewhat, and there had come others. Yet we fought so strenuously with the fear that its headway was but slow, comparatively speaking. We had now given up all thought or hope of leaving the island. We had realized that it would be unallowable to go among healthy humans with the thing from which we were suffering."

"Our food grew scarce after awhile as we had exhausted all the supplies on the ship, and I caught few fish. We were in a sad state and then I made a very horrible discovery. One morning, a little before midday, I came off from the ship with a portion of the biscuits which were left. In the mouth of her tent, I saw my sweetheart sitting, eating something. As I approached, she threw something toward the edge of a little clearing. It fell short, and a vague suspicion having arisen within me, I walked across and picked it up. It was a piece of the gray fungus. She said that her hunger drove her to it. I got her to promise not to touch it again, however great our hunger. After she had promised, she told me that the desire for it had come suddenly, and that until the moment of desire, she had experienced nothing toward it but the most extreme repulsion."

"Later in the day, feeling strangely restless and much shaken with the thing which I had discovered, I made my way along one of the twisted paths where some of the disgusting growths were. I had, once before, ventured along there, but not to any great distance. This time, being involved in perplexing thought, I went much farther."

"Suddenly I heard a queer hoarse sound on my left. Turning quickly, I saw that there was movement among an extraordinarily shaped mass of fungus close to my elbow. It was swaying uneasily, as though it possessed life of its own. Abruptly, as I stared, the thought came to me that the thing had a grotesque resemblance to the figure of a distorted human creature. Even as the this flashed into my brain, there was a slight, sickening noise of tearing, and I saw that one of the branchlike arms was detaching itself from the surrounding masses, and coming toward me. The head of the thing, a grey ball, moved toward me. I stood in terror as the vile arm brushed across my face. I gave out a frightened cry and ran back a few paces. There was a sweetish taste upon my lips where the thing had touched me. I licked them, and was immediately filled with an inhuman desire. I turned and seized a mass of the fungus. I was insatiable. In the midst of devouring, the remembrance of the morning's discovery swept into my brain. I dashed the fragment I held to the ground. Then, I made my way back to the encampment."

"I think she knew, by intuition which love must have given, as soon as she set eyes on me. Her quiet sympathy made it easier for me, and I told her of my sudden weakness, yet omitted to mention the extraordinary thing that had propelled itself toward me. I desired to spare her all unnecessary terror, as she had already endured far too much of it."

"But for myself I had added an intolerable knowledge, to breed an incessant terror in my brain; for I knew that those men from the ship had come onto the island, and that our fate was the same as theirs – to be devoured by desire for the grey plant, and to eventually become what we ate. We try to keep from the abominable food, though the desire for it is sometimes too strong. Yet, day by day, the monstrous fungus devours our bodies. A week ago we ate the last of the biscuits, and since that time I have caught three fish. I was out here fishing when your schooner drifted upon me out of the mist. I hailed you. You know the rest."

There was the dip of an oar. Then the voice came again, and for the last time, sounding through the slight surrounding mist, ghostly and mournful, the pitifully weary man who had endured an unspeakable horror in only a few months, said goodbye.

The morning sun flung a stray beam across the once hidden sea, pierced the mist dully, and lit up the receding boat with a gloomy fire. Indistinctly William saw something nodding between the oars. He thought of a sponge, a great, grey nodding sponge. The oars continued to ply. They were grey, as was the boat, and William's eyes searched a moment vainly for the conjunction of hand and oar. His gaze flashed back to the head. It nodded forward as the oars went backward for the stroke. Then the oars were dipped and the boat, in split second, shot out of sight.

William stood gazing into the distance and he realized where they were. All along the shore he could see ghostlike apparitions flitting into the interior as the sun grew in its morning brightness. The grey fungus was not fungus at all, and it was only grey in the night. In the daylight it was crimson and the despicable things had faces of terror that beckoningly peered outward toward the ship. The man who had rowed to them was the gondolier of death, ship wrecked eons ago on the shore of eternity. The old man was a messenger from Hades, warning them off, but as William looked down on the side of the ship and saw grey fungus working its way up, he knew that he and all his crew were dead, and they had sailed into hell.

Vada Frye's Ghosts in the Darkness of Despair

### Story 8
### Mark's Ghost Story

*One of my grandmother's favourite writers was Mark Twain, or as she frequently called him, Samuel Clemens. She had several copies of Huckleberry Finn and Tom Sawyer scattered around the house, and always told me that I should be reading more Clemens and less Spillane. Alas, my penchant for detective novels made me neglect the higher literary fair for that which I considered more exciting.*

*You could tell her love for Twain by how she often renamed the characters in some of her tales to reflect the characters in his stories or even Mark Twain himself. What follows is one of those stories.*

Mark was in a large room, far up near a place called Camp Butner, in a huge old building whose upper stories had been wholly unoccupied for years, until he came. The place had long been given up to dust and cobwebs, to solitude and silence. It seemed Mark was in a tomb and invading the privacy of the dead that first night he climbed up to his quarters. For the first time in his life a superstitious dread came over him; and as he turned a dark angle of the stairway and a barely visible cobweb swung in his face and clung there, he shuddered as one who had encountered a phantom. Then a man in a white coat passed him.

He was glad enough when he reached his room and locked out the mould and the darkness. A cheery fire was burning in the fireplace, and he sat down before it with a comforting sense of relief. For two hours he sat there, thinking of bygone times; recalling old scenes, and summoning half-forgotten faces out of the mists of the past; listening, in fancy, to voices that long ago grew silent for all time, and to once familiar songs that nobody sings now. And as his reverie softened down to a sadder and sadder pathos, the shrieking of the winds outside softened to a wail, the angry beating of the rain against the panes diminished to a tranquil patter, and one by one the noises outside subsided, until the melancholy cry of a wolf in the distance was the only sound in the night that was now turning darker, and he thought how nice it would be if the rain turned to snow.

The fire had burned low. A sense of loneliness crept over him. He arose and moving stealthily on tiptoe about the room decided to lie down in bed, as if he were around sleeping enemies whose slumbers it would be fatal to break. He covered up in bed, and lay listening to the rain and wind until the sounds lulled him to sleep. He slept profoundly, but how long he did not know. All at once he found himself awake, and filled with a shuddering expectancy. All was still. All but his own heart, which he could actually hear beating. The sheet and blanket on the bed began to slip away slowly toward the foot of the bed, as if someone were pulling them. He could not stir; he could not speak. Still the blankets slipped deliberately away, until his chest was uncovered. Then with a great effort he seized them and drew them over his head. He waited, listened, waited. Once more that steady pull began. At last he was roused by energies and snatched the covers back to their place and held them with a strong grip. He waited. Then, he felt a faint tug, and took a fresh grip. The tug strengthened to a steady strain and grew stronger and stronger. He groaned. An answering groan came from the foot of the bed. Beaded drops of sweat stood upon his forehead. He was more dead than alive. Presently he heard a heavy footstep in the room, but it did not seem human. However, he was relieved as it appeared to be moving away from him. He heard it approach the door and pass out of it without moving bolt or lock and obviously wandered away as he heard the floors creaking outside the room. Then there was silence.

When his excitement subsided, he proclaimed to himself that all this activity was nothing more than a dream. So, he lay thinking it over until he convinced himself that it was a dream, and then a comforting sigh relaxed him. He got up and went over to the door, and when he found that the locks and bolts were just as he had left them, he let out another sigh of relief. He sat down by the fire, when all of a sudden his placid breathing was cut short with a gasp! On the floor by the hearth was soot dust that bore his own bare footprints side by side but there were others, vast in comparison.

He put out the light and returned to bed, shaking with fear. He lay a long time, peering into the darkness and listening. Then he heard a grating noise overhead, like the dragging of a heavy body across the floor; then the throwing down of the body or whatever it was, and the shaking of his windows in response to the concussion. In distant parts of the building he heard the muffled slamming of doors. He heard, at intervals, footsteps creeping in and out among the corridors, and up and down the stairs. Sometimes these noises approached his door, hesitated, and went away again. He heard the clanking of chains faintly, in remote passages, and listened while the clanking grew nearer, as it wearily climbed the stairways, marking each move by the loose surplus of chain that fell with an accented rattle upon each succeeding step as whatever bore it advanced. He heard muttered sentences; half-uttered screams that seemed smothered violently, and the swish of invisible garments, the rush of invisible wings. Then he became conscious that his room was invaded. That he was not alone. He heard sighs and breathings about his bed, and whispering.

## Vada Frye's Ghosts in the Darkness of Despair

Three little spheres of soft light appeared on the ceiling directly over his head, clung and glowed there a moment, and then dropped, two of them upon his face and one upon the left side of the bed. They spattered liquid and felt warm. Intuition told him they had turned to drops of blood as they fell. Then he saw pallid faces, dimly luminous, and white uplifted hands, floating bodiless in the air for a moment and then disappearing. The whispering ceased, as did the voices and the sounds, followed by a solemn stillness. He waited and listened.

Since he had turned off the lights earlier, he was bathed in darkness. He was weak with fear. He slowly raised himself up, and his face came in contact with a clammy hand. All strength went from him, and he fell back as if stricken by a paralysing ray. Then he heard the rustle of a garment, and it seemed to pass to the door and go out.

When everything was still once more, he crept out of bed, sick and feeble, and turned the lights on with a trembling hand. He sat down and fell into a dreamy contemplation of those great footprints in the dust. By and by its outlines began to waver and grow dim. He heard that treading again. He noted its approach, nearer and nearer, along the musty halls, and the lights got dimmer and dimmer. The tread reached his door and paused, the light in the room had now dwindled to mostly a flicker. The door did not open, and yet he felt a faint gust of air fan his cheek, and presently was conscious of a huge, cloudy presence before him. He watched it with fascinated eyes. A pale shimmering glow fell over the thing; gradually its cloudy folds took shape. Mark now knew what it was. It was the man in the white coat.

The morning sun came up and bathed the room in light, as he walked over to the barred window and looked out at a long circular driveway and recalled the chains he had used to kill people, dragging their bodies about with glee. He recalled the one giant of a man he had killed a few years ago – a gentle giant who had shown him pity.

The man in the white coat said, "Now Mark, you are having those delusions again."

Mark looked out at the entrance where a large sign stood glistening in the rising sun, it read: *Camp Butner – Asylum for the Criminally Insane*.

## Story 9
## Machen's March of Death

*Ghosts and apparitions are not always one and the same. My grandmother also loved sharing tales that dealt with what many people would call divine intervention. Seeing an angel is different than seeing a ghost, but, to her, an apparition could be either ghost or angel because she was sceptical of both.*

*She was a young girl during World War I, and recalled well how so many poor farmer's sons were sent off to defeat the German Kaiser, while the sons of the wealthy and powerful were able to avoid service. It was similar to the Vietnam War, which was the era in which I served. Although she died before the Vietnam War was escalated, she told me that, despite my decision to serve, she thought the war was not one which the USA should be fighting. She, despite her meagre education, could not see the wisdom in fighting against a country that simply wanted justice for all*

# Vada Frye's Ghosts in the Darkness of Despair

*its citizens who longed for some economic stability. She saw through the folly of the anti-communist propaganda engaged in by the nation. She saw the enemy of the American people, not as some foreign fighter trying to elevate a nation out of tyranny, but rather as its own government in service to the privileged classes and the corporations. She would not have put it exactly that way, but that is representative of her attitude.*

*Now, she was an avid follower of news from the war front in 1918, when America entered World War I, just as it was winding down. She especially liked the reporting of a man named Machen, who wrote of strange occurrences on the battlefield. What follows is the story as she related to me one Christmas.*

*This affair was such an odd one from first to last, with many unusual complications having entered into it, and many rumours and speculations concerning it that I cannot say categorically that what follows has any foundation in fact; although unlike the previous stories, my grandmother said this was accepted as fact, but only by those with minds that went on blind faith, not cold calculated thought.*

*The story about what happened was retold in several newspapers, and although some, even then, considered it absurd, those with deep faith embraced it with vigour. Regardless of it being truth or fiction, people, especially at the time, took it as an article of faith that the English cause in World War I was just.*

**J. Wayne Frye**

# Vada Frye's Ghosts in the Darkness of Despair

*There are certain psychological morals to be drawn from the whole matter of the tale and its sequel of rumours and discussions that are not, I think, devoid of consequence; and so to thoroughly understand it some readers will have to suspend their rationality, while others, who are of a religious bent will embrace it with no doubts. It does not matter which you are, for what is being told here deals with apparitions, and whether apparitions are ghosts or angels is not as important as the fact that apparitions do appear according to many people. So let us begin just as Vada Frye told it.*

Wayne my boy, in the last Sunday of August 1918, there were terrible things to be read on that hot morning. It was in *The Weekly Dispatch* that I saw the awful account of the retreat from Mons, Belgium. You see, the English had been routed by the Germans and were retreating. I no longer recollect the details after all these years, but I have not forgotten the impression that was then on my mind. I visualized a furnace of torment, death, agony and terror in that awful war. First, all ages and nations have cherished the thought that spiritual hosts may come to the help of earthly beings, that gods and heroes and saints have descended from their high immortal places to fight for their worshippers and clients. The story I am going to tell was printed and reprinted for many years after the war, but is rarely mentioned now.

Many variants of the tale began to be told as authentic histories, but what I am going to tell is as close to the truth as I know it. I, frankly, do not believe it, but it is up to you to decide for yourself. Many of these variations betrayed their relation to the original.

The retreat of eighty thousand men at the first battle of Mon was on the most awful day of that awful time; a day when ruin and disaster came so near that its shadow fell over the entire British Empire. On this dreadful day, then, when three hundred thousand German men in arms with all their artillery swelled like a flood against the little English company of men trapped in Mon there was one point above all other points in the battle line that was for a time in awful danger, not merely of defeat, but of utter annihilation. That morning the German guns had thundered and shrieked against the town of Mon, and against the thousand or so men who held it. The men joked at the shells, and found funny names for them, and had bets about them, and greeted them with songs. But the shells came on and burst, and tore good Englishmen limb from limb, and as the heat of the day increased so did the fury of that terrific bombardment. There was no help it seemed. The English artillery was good, but there was not nearly enough of it; it was being steadily battered into scrap iron.

There comes a moment in a storm at sea when people say to one another that it is at its worst; it can blow no harder, and then there is a blast ten times more fierce than any before. So it was in these British trenches and the town of Mon.

**J. Wayne Frye**

# Vada Frye's Ghosts in the Darkness of Despair

There were no stouter hearts in the whole world than the hearts of these men; but even they were appalled at this hell that fell upon them, overwhelmed them and destroyed them. And at this very moment they saw from their trenches that a tremendous host was moving against their lines. Only five hundred of the thousand remained, and as far as they could see the German infantry was pressing on against them, column upon column, a grey wall of men, ten thousand of them, as it was admitted to afterward by the Germans, themselves. There was no hope at all. They shook hands, some of them, for they knew the end was near.

Many of the men of that day were far more religious than those you find today, and many began to pray. A group of Catholics began praying to St. George. How ironic that as they prayed to a saint who would have been by Jesus' side, the Prince of Peace, these very men were firing frantically at the advancing Germans, killing scores of them.

One lone particularly devout man behind a burned out tank uttered his invocation loud enough for even the Germans to hear and suddenly he felt something between a shudder and an electric shock pass through his body. The roar of the battle died down in his ears to a gentle murmur; instead of it, he says, he heard a great voice and a shout louder than a thunder-peal crying, "Array, array, array!"

His heart grew hot as a burning coal, as it seemed to him that a tumult of voices answered to his summons. He heard voices in unison shouting "St. George, St. George."

Someone else called out – "St. George, heaven's knight, the bowmen so strong, help us."

And as the soldier heard these voices, he saw before him, beyond the trench, a long line of shapes, with a shining about them. They were like men who drew the bow, and with another shout their cloud of arrows flew singing and tingling through the air towards the German hosts. The other men in the trench were firing all the while. Suddenly one of them lifted up his voice in the plainest English, "God help us!" he bellowed to the man next to him, and then someone shouted "but we're blooming marvels of shot. Look at those grey bastards, look at them! All dying, see them? They're not going down in dozens, nor in hundreds; it's thousands, it is. Look! Look! There's a regiment gone while I'm talking to you."

"Shut it!" another soldier bellowed, taking aim, "what are you talking about! They come. They come." But he gulped with astonishment even as he spoke, for, indeed, the grey men were falling by the thousands. The English could hear the guttural scream of the German officers, the crackle of their revolvers as they shot the reluctant; and still line after line crashed to the earth. The singing arrows fled so swift and thick that they darkened the air as the horde melted from before them. While some were shouting miracle, others kept firing.

Within a few minutes, there were ten thousand dead German soldiers. In Germany, a country ruled by scientific principles, it was assumed that the contemptible English must have employed shells containing an unknown gas of a poisonous nature, as so many men were found dead, but no wounds were discernible on the bodies of so many German soldiers. But for many of the English, it was St. George had brought his ancient bowmen to help slay the Germans.

Now, no one on the German side ever mentioned anything about what happened, because there were none to tell it from their side as they were all dead, but many of the English said they saw an army of bowmen marching in a mist toward the Germans. Others said they saw nothing, except that the Germans just seemed to fall before the fusillade of bullets.

One English soldier said that he saw many ghostly looking spectres in a mist march toward the German soldiers, and a few supported his story. It should be known that pressing the belief that God was on England's side was good for morale, so the officers and politicians supported this story and promoted it.

I am not saying one way or the other, but I can tell you that there were no arrows found on the battlefield, and no wounds found on many of the Germans that indicated they were shot by an arrow. Of course, several of the soldiers said that the arrows that were fired from the silver bows seemed to be like mists that penetrated the soldiers who fell precariously forward. In fact, most of the dead Germans were found lying face down.

## Vada Frye's Ghosts in the Darkness of Despair

One must admit that it is a bit unusual that most of the dead would fall face forward. As mentioned, the Germans accused the British of using some kind of secret poison weapon. There has never been any corroboration of that by anyone in all these years.

An intrepid reporter named Machen covered the story and interviewed many of the British soldiers, but he got conflicting accounts, but being a very religious man, he put more credence in the account of apparitions appearing on the battlefield.

A few years ago, battlefield historians were digging in the old Mon battlefield, and they found several skeletons, assumed to be German. Two of the skeletons were turned over to forensic scientists who found something very interesting. There was no indication of bullet wounds, but rather, their breast bones had the markings that indicated they had been shot with arrows that penetrated the hearts.

## Story 10
## The Field of Poppies

*For some reason, my grandmother was fascinated by World War I, despite the fact her own son (my father) had served in the military in World War II, along with so many people she knew. Perhaps, it was because she was such a young girl at the time that it made more of an impression on her. I often queried her about whether or not she had a beau who served, but she always was non-committal in reply. I wonder if it was perhaps because she had lost someone she loved dearly to that war, as, like most wars, the government somehow seemed to pluck boys from the direst economic circumstances to do the fighting and dying. How ironic that those who usually do the fighting and dying to defend democracy and the great American way seem to be the least of the beneficiaries in that great democracy. Nonetheless, here is another one of my favourites that she shared about World War I.*

## Vada Frye's Ghosts in the Darkness of Despair

The soldier with the ugly wound in the head opened his eyes at last, and looked about him with an air of pleasant satisfaction. He still felt drowsy and dazed after the fierce experience through which he had passed, but so far he could not recollect much about it. However, an agreeable glow began to steal about him, such a glow as comes to people who have been in a tight spot and have come through it better than they had expected.

The wounded soldier opened his eyes, pulled himself together, and looked about him. He felt a sense of delicious ease and repose in bones that had been racked and weary, and deep in the heart that had so lately been tormented there was an assurance of comfort, of a battle being won. After fatigues and terrors that as yet he could not recollect he seemed now to be resting in a chair in a dim, low-lit room.

In the hearth there was a glint of fire and a blue, sweet-scented puff of wood smoke; a great black oak beam roughly hewn crossed the ceiling. Through the leaded panes of the windows he saw a rich glow of sunlight, green lawns, and against the deepest and most radiant of all blue skies the wonderful far-lifted towers of a vast, mystic, rich with imagery gate opening into a beautiful field of poppies.

"How magnificent." he murmured to himself. He dozed off again, thinking they should call the place *Soldier's Rest* as it was so tranquil, peaceful and beautiful.

# Vada Frye's Ghosts in the Darkness of Despair

After a brief sleep, he opened his eyes and a man in a black cassock was standing by him. The man said, "Are you all right now?"

"Yes, thank you, sir, as right as can be. I hope to be back to the front again soon," he replied.

"Well, right now relax, you have earned a rest," replied the man in the black robe. He continued, as he pointed to his head wound, "Where did you get that?"

The soldier put his hand up to his brow, looking dazed and puzzled. "Well, sir," he said, "it was like this, to begin at the beginning. An awful time it was, and I don't know how I got through it alive. My best friend was killed dead beside me as we lay in the street. That I remember well, but the rest is a bit foggy. I do recall about a dozen of us in the village, and two or three hundred Germans came down on us early one morning. They got us good they did. We were captured you know. They tied our hands behind our backs, and smacked our faces and kicked us a bit, and we were lined up opposite the house where we'd been hiding. And then that poor little chap broke away from his mother, and he run out and saw one of the Germans hit me one over the jaw with his clenched fist. Oh dear! Oh dear! He might have done it a dozen times if only that little child hadn't seen him. The boy was no more than three and kept shouting in French, "Bad man! Bad man!"

The soldier then hung his head and said, "The damn German took his bayonet and rammed the blade through the poor boy's neck."

## Vada Frye's Ghosts in the Darkness of Despair

The recollections were causing him pain. The soldier's face worked and twitched and twisted itself into a grimace, and he sat grinding his teeth and staring at the man in the black robe. He was silent for a little. And then he found his voice, and the oaths rolled terrible, thundering from him, as he cursed that murderous wretch, and bade him go down and burn for ever in hell. And the tears were raining down his face, and they choked him at last. "I beg your pardon, sir, I'm sure," he said, "especially you being a minister or priest, I suppose; but I can't help it, he was such a dear little boy and the cruelty of murdering him for no real reason."

The man in black murmured "In the sight of the Lord is the death of His innocents." Then he put a hand very gently on the soldier's shoulder, patting him lightly. "You have seen horrors my boy, but I worry about your wound. Are you comfortable here?"

"Oh, that; that's nothing. But I'll tell you how I got it. It was just like this. The Germans had us fair, as I tell you, and they shut us up in a barn in the village; just flung us on the ground and left us to starve seemingly. They barred up the big door of the barn, and put a sentry there, and thought we were all right. There were sort of slits like very narrow windows in one of the walls, and on the second day it was, I was looking out of these slits down the street, and I could see those German devils were up to mischief. They were planting their machine-guns everywhere an ordinary man coming up the street would never see them, but I saw them, and I saw the infantry lining up behind the garden walls. Then I had a sort of a notion of what was coming; and presently, sure enough, I could hear some of our chaps singing in the distance, and I told myself that they had to be warned. So I looked about me, and I found a hole under the wall, a kind of a drain I should think it was, and I found I could just squeeze through. And I got out and crept round and away with my friend behind me, both of us running down the street, yelling, just as our chaps were getting around the corner at the bottom of the hill. Bang, bang went the guns, behind me and in front of me, and on each side of me, and then I see my friend's head explode from a fusillade of bullets from the machine guns. Something hit me on the head and over I went; and I don't remember anything more until I woke up here just now."

The soldier lay back in his chair and closed his eyes for a moment. When he opened them, he saw that there were other people in the room besides the minister in the black robe. One was a man in a big black, long, flowing cloak. He had a grim old face and a great beaky nose. He shook the soldier by the hand as he said, "Wake up boy."

Then, someone came out of the shadow, someone in queer clothes such as the soldier had seen worn by old guards at Buckingham Palace. "Of all knights you be noblest and gentlest, and you be of fairest report, and now you be a brother of the noblest brotherhood that ever was since this world's beginning."

The soldier did not understand what the man was saying to him. There were others, too, in strange dresses, who came and spoke to him. Some spoke in what sounded like French, even German. He could not make it out; but he knew that they all spoke kindly and praised him.

"What does it all mean?" he said to the minister. "What are they talking about? They don't think I'd let down my pals?"

"Drink this," said the minister, and he handed the soldier a great silver cup, brimming with wine. The soldier took a long drink, and in that moment all his sorrows passed from him.

"What is it?" he asked?

Then, the minister bent down and murmured in the soldier's ear: "That is the elixir of eternity my boy." Then the black robe seemed to melt away and was replaced with a shiny, white cassock as the man took his hand, pulling him up while softly saying as they walked toward the gate that opened into the field of poppies, "You are but a ghost my boy at the way station to eternity. Come, join your friend who waits on the other side in the field of poppies."

## Story 11
## The Church Bell

*Winters in my North Carolina childhood were colder than today. (Yes, global warming is real!) Perhaps it was the cold of winter that bred the desire to hear of misery, of lost hope, of things that go bump in the night, as it was a time of contemplative thought and reflection. Listening to grandmother tell a ghost story, as snowflakes fell faintly through the night was like a descent into purgatory. We all must face death. It is inevitable. However, our journey, though often arduous and fraught with disappointment, is one that can lead to a life of hope. Many times I have lost hope, but somehow struggled to find it again. The older people get, the more they seem to lose hope, looking back on lives they think were not as meaningful as they should have been, but simply surviving to old age is an accomplishment in a world filled with far too much hate and indifference. Survival is victory!*

# Vada Frye's Ghosts in the Darkness of Despair

*My grandmother loved Twain, but she also enjoyed Hawthorne, so she would often regale people with stories that she said were inspired by Hawthorne's short forays into maddening mayhem of the mind. (How's that for alliteration?) Here is one she shared with me often.*

There is a certain church, in the country which I have always regarded with peculiar interest. It is a stately church surrounded by an enclosure of the loveliest green, within which appear urns, pillars, obelisks, and other forms of monumental marble.

There was a marriage there by a woman twice married before and a man who had practiced years of celibacy it was said. At sixty-five, Mr. Ellenwood was a shy but not quite a secluded man; selfish, yet manifesting on rare occasions a vein of generous sentiment; a scholar throughout life, though always an indolent one, because his studies had no definite object either of public advantage or personal ambition; a gentleman, high-bred and fastidiously delicate, yet sometimes requiring a considerable relaxation in his behalf of the common rules of society. In truth, there were so many anomalies in his character, and, though shrinking with diseased sensibility from public notice, it had been his fatality so often to become the topic of the day by some wild eccentricity of conduct, that people searched his lineage for a hereditary taint of insanity. But there was no need of this. His caprices had their origin in a mind that lacked an engrossing purpose. If he were mad, it was the consequence of an aimless life.

**J. Wayne Frye**

## Vada Frye's Ghosts in the Darkness of Despair

The widow he was to marry was as complete a contrast to her third bridegroom in everything but age, being nearly 60, herself. Her first husband, nearly twice her age, had killed himself, leaving her in possession of a splendid fortune. Her second husband was considerably younger than she, but within 3 years, he, too died. Thus, she went many years without a close male companion as she assumed she was not meant for marital blissfulness. To be brief, she was that wisest but un-loveliest variety of woman. However, she seemed to simply refuse to grow old and ugly on any consideration. She struggled with time, but the struggle went well for her.

The approaching marriage of this worldly woman, Clara Dabney, to Eben Ellenwood, was announced soon after she arrived back in the little town of Denton, after having spent many years in Charlotte. Superficial observers, and deeper ones, seemed to concur in supposing that the lady must have borne no inactive part in arranging the affair, despite there being what appeared as little romance in this late union. All the wonder was how the gentleman, with his lack of worldly wisdom was suitable for Clara. As the marriage was about to be solemnized, many spectators occupied the front seats of the galleries and the pews near the altar. It had been arranged, or possibly it was the custom of the day, that the parties should proceed separately to church. By some accident the bridegroom was a little less punctual than the widow and her bridal attendants, with whose arrival the action of this tale may be said to commence.

The ladies composing the bride's party came through the church door with the sudden effect of a burst of sunshine and stepped to the right into an ante-room to await the arrival of the groom. The whole group, except the principal figure, was made up of young girls. As they stood in the ante-room, the pews and pillars seemed to brighten on either side as the people gathered there awaiting the groom's entrance. So brilliant was the spectacle that few took notice of a singular phenomenon that had marked the bride's entrance. At the moment when the bride's foot touched the threshold, the bell swung heavily in the church tower above her and sent forth its deepest knell. The vibrations died away, and returned with prolonged solemnity as she entered the church and walked to the side room.

One person was heard to whisper, "Why did the infernal bell ring? It is only rung for funerals." Alas, most there saw its ringing as a bad omen.

The bride and her company had been too much occupied with the bustle of entrance to hear the first boding stroke of the bell, or, at least, to reflect on the uncanny nature of such a welcome to the altar. Suddenly, there was another stroke of the bell that seemed to fill the church with a visible gloom, dimming and obscuring the bright pageant.

This time the bride's party wavered and huddled closer together, while a slight sigh was heard from some of the brides' maids and a confused whispering among the people in the church as the bell continued to swing, strike and vibrate with the same doleful regularity as when a corpse is on its way to the tomb.

The minister whispered to an altar boy to see who was ringing that infernal bell. A brief space elapsed as the bell continued to ring at varying intervals of about 30 seconds. Now, beside the church was the cemetery where Clara's two previous husbands were buried. The widow's glance was observed to wander for an instant toward a window, as her thoughts were drawn irresistibly to the two graves in the graveyard that adjoined the church. Still, the death-bell tolled so mournfully that the sunshine seemed to fade in the air. A whisper, communicated from those who stood nearest the windows, now spread through the church: a hearse with a train of several coaches was creeping along the street, conveying some dead man to the churchyard, while the bride awaited a living one. Immediately after, the footsteps of the bridegroom and his friends were heard at the door. The widow looked down the aisle and clenched the arm of one of her brides' maids in her bony hand with such unconscious violence that the fair girl trembled.

"You frighten me, Clara," cried the woman. "For heaven's sake, what is wrong? What is my dear?"

"Nothing," said the widow; then, whispering close to her ear, "There is a foolish fancy that I cannot get rid of. I am expecting my bridegroom to come into the church with my two first husbands for groomsmen."

"Look!" screamed the bride's maid. "What is here? A funeral!"

As she spoke a dark procession paced into the church. First came an old man and woman, like chief mourners at a funeral, attired from head to foot in the deepest black, all but their pale features and stringy hair, he leaning on a staff and supporting her decrepit form with his boney arm, while behind appeared another and another pair, as aged, as black and mournful as the first. As they drew near, the widow recognized in every face some trait of former friends long forgotten, but now returning as if from their old graves to warn her to prepare a shroud, or, with purpose almost as unwelcome, to exhibit their wrinkles and infirmity and claim her as their companion by the tokens of her own decay. Many a merry night had she danced with them in youth, and now in joyless age she felt that some withered partner should request her hand and all unite in a dance of death to the music of the funeral-bell which was still ringing.

As these aged mourners were passing up the aisle it was observed that from pew to pew the spectators shuddered with irrepressible awe as some object hitherto concealed by the intervening figures came full in sight. Many turned away their faces; others kept a fixed and rigid stare, and a young girl giggled hysterically. When the spectral procession approached the altar, each couple separated and slowly diverged, until in the centre appeared a form that had been worthily ushered in with all this gloomy pomp, the death-knell and the funeral. It was the bridegroom in his shroud.

No garb but that of the grave could have befitted such a death-like aspect. The eyes were fixed in the stern calmness which old men wear in the coffin. The corpse stood motionless, turned back toward the ante-room and said, "Come, my bride! The hearse is ready to take us on the honeymoon in the churchyard tomb. Let us be married, and then to our coffins!"

How shall the widow's horror be represented? It gave her the ghastliness of a dead man's bride. Her youthful friends stood apart, shuddering at the mourners, the shrouded bridegroom and herself; the whole scene expressed by the strongest imagery the vain struggle of the gilded vanities of this world when opposed to age, infirmity, sorrow and death.

The awestruck silence was first broken by the minister, who was amazed at the obvious charade as he said, "Mr. Ellenwood, this is a travesty. You are not well. Your mind has been agitated by the unusual circumstances in which you are placed. The ceremony is not going forward. You should go home."

"Home, yes; but not without my dear bride," he answered, as he continued; "you deem this mockery, perhaps madness. I say no."

He stepped forward at a ghostly pace and stood beside the far widow, contrasting the awful simplicity of his shroud with the glare and glitter in which his bride, now standing in the aisle near the altar in her beautiful, colourful gown.

He then pointed at his bride-to-be. "In youth you deprived me of my happiness, my hopes, my aims; you took away all the substance of my life and made it a dream without reality, only providing a gloom, through which I walked wearily and cared not even for life. I know you killed your first husband with poison so you could inherit his wealth. How do I know? You once whispered of it in your sleep, but I knew I could never prove it."

Then he pointed at the graveyard and the tomb where her second husband was supposed to be buried. "There I am supposed to lie, but I do not. All assumed I killed myself, and you buried an empty coffin, because when I heard you utter the truth of your treachery in your sleep, I determined that I must escape your evil, before I too met the same fate as your first husband. I have been gone 30 years, but I come back here now to say to all – you are a murderous fiend."

Clara turned and ran from the church as if the devil himself was at her back. She scurried across the cemetery, and as she approached the grave of her first husband, she stumbled on a raised portion of earth, hitting her head on the tombstone as she fell. As blood streamed out of the gapping wound that had crushed her skull, the church bell rang again and again and again.

## Story 12
## The Portrait of the Lady in the Velvet Gown

*There will be even those today who will ridicule the story that follows as we live in a world where the paragons of virtue want to force all of us into the same, staid mould of conformity. However, it is here, because I believe in love in all its forms. This is a story of unusual love, especially for the time (Victorian England) in which it took place. However, for those who think love is only reserved for the sanctified, my grandmother, a woman far ahead of her time would have said, "poppycock." This was always one of my favourite stories, because frankly, it titillated me. After all, when she first told it to me, I was a budding adolescent with raging hormones. As the saying goes, "save the best for last."*

To be rich is a luxurious sensation, the more so when you have plumbed the depths of poverty. Edith Nesbitt had been to the bottom, scraping by on a cub reporter's pay at a small newspaper.

# Vada Frye's Ghosts in the Darkness of Despair

However, when her Aunt Dora died and left her a monthly stipend for life, she felt that life had nothing left to offer except immediate possession of the good things. Even Manfred Mayhew, whom she had hitherto regarded as her life's light, became less luminous. She was not engaged to Manfred, but she lodged with his mother, and loved singing duets with him. He was a dear good man, and she meant to marry him some day. Still, her inheritance almost put Manfred out of her head, especially as she was now in a luxurious country mansion. She was seated in her aunt's armchair in front of the fire in the living room of the house, which she had strangely never visited for her aunt had also kept a city place for as long as Edith could remember. She had often wondered why her aunt never had her visit there.

The room was comfortably furnished with antiques. On the walls hung a few fairly good oil paintings, but the space above the mantelpiece was disfigured by an exceedingly horrible print in a beautiful dark frame. She got up to look at it. She had always thought her aunt a woman of good taste, but this thing was hideous. The ornate frame was not intended for a print, but for an oil-painting. It was of fine ebony, beautifully and curiously carved. She looked at it with growing interest, and when her aunt's housemaid came in, as she had retained the two servants, she asked her how long the print had been there?

"I only bought it two days before she got ill," she said; "but the frame, she didn't want to buy a new one, so she got this out of the attic. There are lots of curious old things up there."

"Did my aunt have this frame long?"

"Oh, yes. It must have come long before I did, and I've been here seven years come Christmas. There was a picture in it. That's upstairs too, but it's so black and ugly."

For some reason, she felt compelled to see the picture. What if it were some priceless old masterpiece, in which her aunt's eyes had only seen rubbish? So, directly after breakfast next morning, she paid a visit to the attic. It was crammed with old furniture, enough to stock an antique shop. Tables with mother-of-pearl inlays, straight-backed chairs, needle-work cushions, and gilded carvings abounded.

She promised herself a good time in placing these household goods in her own parlour. Still, she needed to find that picture. With the housemaid, Jane, by her side, she quickly found it behind some rubbish. Neither subject nor colour was distinguishable. There was a splash of a darker tint in the middle, but whether it was figure, or tree, or house, no one could have told. It seemed to be painted on a very thick panel bound with leather. She thought of sending it to a restorer, but as she gazed at its obvious lack of worth, she determined to try her own hand at its restoration.

She immediately set to the task with soap and nail polish but found in a hurry that there was no picture to clean. Bare oak presented itself to her persevering brush. She tried the other side, Jane watching her with indulgent interest. The same result. Then the truth dawned on her. Why was the panel so thick? She tore off the leather binding, and the panel divided and fell to the ground in a cloud of dust. There were two pictures; they had been nailed face to face. She leaned them against the wall. She was astonished that one of the pictures was of her, a perfect portrait, and no shade of expression or turn of feature not done to absolute perfection. When had this been done, she thought, as she had no recollection of ever sitting for a portrait. Jane was puzzled too, as she stood staring, seemingly mesmerized by what was there before them.

Jane said, "You are very beautiful in this miss. When was it done?"

Quizzically, Edith shook her head as she said, "I have no recollection of sitting for it. I do not know."

After awhile, Jane left Edith alone and she turned, still with her heart beating violently, to the other picture. This was a beautiful woman with a straight nose, low brows, full lips, thin hands, large, deep, luminous eyes. She wore a black velvet gown. It was a three-quarter-length portrait. Her arms rested on a table beside her and her head on her hands; but her face was turned full forward, and her eyes met those of the spectator bewilderingly. On the table by her were compasses and shining instruments whose uses Edith did not know, books and a heap of papers and pens. It was nearly a quarter of an hour before she could turn her eyes from the picture. She had never seen such mesmerizing, commanding eyes as those possessed by the lady in the portrait.

She proceeded downstairs, tore down the disgusting looking cheap print and put the picture of the woman in its strong ebony frame. Then she wrote to a frame-maker for a frame for her own portrait. The new frame came, and she hung it opposite the fireplace. An exhaustive search among her aunt's papers showed no explanation of the portrait of herself, no history of the portrait of the woman with the wonderful eyes. She only learned that all the old furniture together had come to her aunt at the death of her great-uncle, the head of the family; and she should have concluded that the resemblance was only a family one, if everyone who came in had not exclaimed at the similarities.

She invited her boyfriend and his mother to visit her in the near future; and, for some reason, she avoided glancing at the picture in the ebony frame. She could not forget, nor remember without singular emotion, the look in the eyes of that woman when hers first met them. She had trepidation about looking into them again.

She reorganised the house somewhat, preparing for her new guests. She brought down much of the old-fashioned furniture, and after a long day of arranging and re-arranging, she sat down before the fire, and lying back in a pleasant languor, she idly raised her eyes to the picture of the woman.

# Vada Frye's Ghosts in the Darkness of Despair

She met her dark, deep, hazel eyes, and once more her gaze was held fixed as by magic, the kind of fascination that keeps one sometimes staring for whole minutes into one's own eyes in the glass. She gazed into her eyes, and felt her own dilate with tears.

Then, she whispered, "I wish you were a woman and not a picture! Come down! Ah, come down!" She laughed at herself as she spoke; but even as she laughed, she outstretched her arms as if beckoning her. Then she saw the eyes of the woman dilate, her lips tremble. Her hands moved slightly; and a sort of flicker of a smile passed over her face. She leapt to her feet, stood there and thought that the firelight was playing strange tricks. She was stunned at her imagination. Yes, it was her imagination.

She heard a sound behind her in the dimness of the room. The fire had burned low and the corners of the room were deeply shadowed; but there, behind the tall Queen Ann Chair, was something darker than a shadow. She seized the fireplace poker, and battered the dull coals to a blaze. Then she stepped back resolutely, and looked at the picture. The ebony frame was empty! From the shadow of the chair came a soft rustle, and out of the shadow the woman of the picture was coming, coming towards her.

She could not move or even scream. She thought that all the known laws of nature were nothing, or she was mad. She stood trembling while the woman in the black velvet gown swept across the

**J. Wayne Frye**

hearthrug towards her. The next moment a hand touched her, a hand, soft, warm, and human, and a low voice said, "You called me. I am here."

At that touch and that voice, the world seemed to give a sort of bewildering half-turn. She hardly knew how to express it, but at once it seemed not awful, not even unusual, for portraits to become flesh, only most natural, most right and most unspeakably fortunate. She laid her hand on hers. The woman looked over at Edith's portrait. She could not see it in the firelight as Edith said, "We are not strangers."

The woman replied, "Oh, no, not strangers," as those luminous eyes stared directly at Edith.

With a passionate cry, a sense of having recovered life's most precious gift, she clasped the lady in her arms. She was no ghost; she was a woman, the only woman in the world.

"How long," Edith said, "how long is it since I lost you?"

She leaned back, hanging her full weight on the heels of her feet as the lady replied softly "How can I tell how long? There is no time in hell."

It was not a dream. Ah! No. There are no such dreams in this world. It is very difficult to tell a story of forbidden love, but it must be told. There are no words to express the sense of glad reunion, the complete realization of every hope and dream of a life that came upon her as she sat glaring into her eyes.

She fetched wood for the fire as the woman sat still. You could see the love in her dear eyes;

when she threw herself by her side and blessed the day she was born. Not a thought of her Manfred entered her brain; all other things in her life were a dream, this splendid thing before her was reality.

"You remember nothing? Really nothing?" said the lady in black velvet.

The reply was filled with love. "Only that I am truly yours; that we have both suffered; that, tell me, my darling dear, all that you remember. Explain it all to me. Make me understand. And yet? No, I don't want to understand. It is enough that we are together."

She leaned towards Edith, her arm lay on her neck, and she drew Edith's head until it rested on her shoulder. "I am a ghost, I suppose," she said, laughing softly; and her laughter stirred memories which Edith just grasped at and just missed. "But you and I know better, don't we? I will tell you everything you have forgotten. We loved each other. Our pictures were painted before you went away. The church drove you away, because of our forbidden love, insisted that your aunt separate us, make us deny that which made us whole. You were sent to an asylum for the insane, where people who dared love unconventionally were often placed in shock therapy to calm them into submission and to cleanse their brains of unwanted thoughts, unwanted by the virtuous controllers who point with the finger of condemnation. Finally, after many years you put my memory into the dark recesses of your mind. How can it be a sin to love? Does not the accursed church preach of a man who abided with love for all? Would he have not sanctified our love, our commitment to one another? Oh, how I longed for you. I walked in a comatose state for days longing to hold you in my arms again. Alas, I could endure the pain no longer when told you would never leave the asylum. I took a rope and hanged myself from the beam on the front porch."

Edith was crying now, as a flood of memories flowed in sweet tears that floated gently down her cheek. The lady in velvet continued, "Many years went by as you endured the hell of the asylum, and one night when my mother, your aunt, sat right here before my picture, she wept and cried about how two female cousins could love each other in such a forbidden way, pleading with me to come back. And I went to her with glad leaps of heart. Oh, but she shrank from me, she fled and she shrieked and moaned of ghosts. She had our pictures covered from sight, and put again in the ebony frame. She had promised me my picture should stay always there. Ah, through all these years your sweet face was against mine. I can taste your sweetness still."

"Why," Edith asked, "did I not remember all this? How could I ever forget such a love? But I remember now. Oh yes, I remember all our joy."

Day dawned and Jane came into the parlour where Edith sat there alone. She walked over to her and reached down to arouse her from sleep. But she would not arouse her from this sleep, for it was eternal.

## Vada Frye's Ghosts in the Darkness of Despair

Many years have passed and the home was torn down, but there was a portrait that was found in the attic by the wrecking crew, and today it hangs in a London museum. It is a portrait of two women sitting on a sofa, smiling at one another with love.

# Vada Frye's Ghosts in the Darkness of Despair

## Epilogue
## Yes We Were

It has been many years since my grandmother passed away, but like the portraits in the prior story, our love knows no constraints in the cosmos of time. As a non-believer, I do not pray, but I do lie in bed, as I have every night since her death, and say before going to sleep that I am thankful for the love we shared. The stories she told me helped stimulate my creativity, and though by no means a highly successful writer, I do enjoy a modicum of recognition that gives me great pleasure.

My grandmother's daughter, Willa Mae, was a woman I loved almost as much as my grandmother, because she was imbued with the same kindness, compassion and magnificence that made you feel as if you were in the presence of an angel. A few years before her death, she came to visit me at my chateau high on a hill on Vancouver Island in Canada, where my office looked out upon the ocean and the towering mountains of the mainland in the distance. As we sat talking, we shared so many of the wonderful memories of Vada Frye, her mother and my grandmother. She turned to me and said with conviction, "I love you Wayne, but you know what, sometimes I was a little jealous of you, because my mother loved you so much, but I realize now that you needed her love more than anybody. We were both so lucky to have been loved by such an extraordinary woman."

# YES WE WERE!

## Vada Frye's Ghosts in the Darkness of Despair

**If you liked these thrilling ghost stories,
do not miss the other J. Wayne Frye tales
of the supernatural.**

*Lynton Buys a New Cell Phone
And
Hears the Voice of Doom*

*Lynton and the Vampire at Tagaytay Manor*

*Lynton Viñas and Beowulf Perez:
Demon Fighters In the Taal Inferno*

*Lynton and the Ghosts
At
The Mansion on Balete Drive*

*Lynton Viñas: Shadow in the Darkness*

*Something Evil in the Darkness
At
Hopkins House*